To

Charl

Follow Me

Victoria Gemmell

I hope you enjoy!

Best wishes,

Victoria Gemmell x

Published by
Strident Publishing Ltd
22 Strathwhillan Drive
The Orchard
Hairmyres
East Kilbride
G75 8GT

Tel: +44 (0)1355 220588
info@stridentpublishing.co.uk
www.stridentpublishing.co.uk

Published by Strident Publishing, 2015

Cover photography & design by Ida Henrich

Poetry quotations
She Walks in Beauty by Lord Byron, page 135
Ode on a Grecian Urn by John Keats, pages 162-163
The Lady of Shalott by Alfred, Lord Tennyson, page 191

A catalogue record for this book is available from the British Library.

ISBN 978-1-910829-03-5

Typeset in Optima by Andrew Forteath | Printed by Bell & Bain

The publisher acknowledges support from Creative Scotland towards the publication of this title.

For my mum, dad and brother, who have always encouraged my creativity

PROLOGUE

We were Gemini Twins, my sister and I. Two halves making up one whole. She always said I took on all of the darker characteristics of the sign, moody and introverted. She was the sunshine to my darkness; outgoing and full of laughter. I dyed my hair black and matched my foundation to the colour of snow. Her hair shone of gold and she always had a smile on her face. She was the happy one.

It made her suicide all the more shocking.

My parents turned to me for answers. I wasn't sure, but I thought I saw a trace of accusation in their eyes. Had my darkness seeped into her light and tainted her sunny disposition?

I only had one answer: my beautiful carefree sister would not take her own life. She was not distraught or desperate.

She was also not the only one to go. Our town almost didn't react to the news of her death. Everyone was slowly switching off, becoming numb, as Abby became another haunting statistic.

Over the past year there had been other teenage suicides in our town. Abby was number five. None of them left suicide notes and none of them said goodbye to their loved ones. *Why*? It was the only question I had. I screamed it over and over in my head every minute of every day.

CHAPTER 1

There was a chilling silence in the corridors at school as if death was hiding around every corner. I walked past people in a daze, feeling like I had left my insides at home, back in the haven of my bedroom. I pulled at my trousers, only half conscious that they were slipping down. I couldn't remember the last time I'd managed to eat a full meal. Food no longer had a taste. Everything was sawdust, everything was grey.

"Hi Kat." Sarah was waiting for me at my locker. Her eyes darted to the side, towards Abby's locker. Her name was still there, written in black marker inside a Tipp-Ex heart. Sarah noticed I had followed her gaze and immediately looked ashamed.

"Hi," I said, opening my locker and shoving my books inside. "How was your summer?"

"Okay," she nodded. She looked at me, chewing on her lip.

A horrible pain twisted in my chest. I wanted her to say *something* but I didn't know *what* I wanted her to say.

The bell rang.

"I've got English, I'd better go… See you at lunch?" she said.

"Yeah. See you." I watched as she dashed off, practically running.

Crowds walked past in slow motion. Kids cast glances in my direction. They kept their distance, like death was a disease that I'd been in contact with and they didn't want to catch it.

I waited until the crowds dispersed into classrooms before I moved. Walking down the corridor, every noticeboard I passed had an advert for some sort of counselling. A new afterschool youth group, a lunchtime drop in, one-to-one appointments with a professional counsellor based in the school…a leaflet for the

Samaritans.

I wondered if the local council and the government had employed people to post them up in the school over the holidays. They had to be seen to be doing *something*. That was what I kept hearing people say.

"Kat."

I turned round and my guidance teacher, Miss Rowan, was standing smiling at me. "It's good to see you back."

"Thanks," I said.

"Want me to walk you to your first class?" she offered.

"No, that's okay." I shook my head. I didn't want to admit that I couldn't remember what my first class was.

"I was so proud when I saw your exam results. All that hard work paid off; I knew it would."

I nodded.

"Not only were you the only 5th year to get five As but they were really high bands too, Kat."

My heart did a little jump. Five As.

She stepped forward and looked me in the eye. "I know you're in a lot of pain, pet. But you should be really proud." She touched my arm and it felt like an electric shock. "Come and see me anytime. Anything you want to talk about I'm here to listen." She smiled and then walked off. Tears stung my eyes and I blinked them away, determined I wasn't going to cry here.

I stood looking at the walls, my eyes following the cracks of paint and chips in the plasterboard. It had always been my plan to stay on for a 6th year to achieve more Highers to ensure my place at uni for Law. I never expected to get five As in the one go. I took a few more steps forward, hesitated, then walked back down to the lockers.

I traced a finger round the heart circling Abby's name. There were too many memories of her here, just like at home. Abby always liked to fill blank sheets of paper with hearts and intricate flowers; the notebook beside the phone decorated with her doodles. I should have told her how great she was at drawing, instead of dismissing everything she did and liked as too girly.

I turned the combination of her locker; our birthday. I was disappointed but not surprised to find it empty inside. I knew Mum and Dad had been and taken her stuff away to trawl through for clues, still searching for an explanation as to why she took her life. The police had got involved a bit, bowing to political pressure and press speculation that something sinister must be going on. I kept asking them if they'd found anything. They kept telling us, 'nothing of any great significance'.

I slammed the locker shut, the sound echoing down the corridor. I didn't want to be there. I started to run, my boots clicking faster and faster until I reached the main entrance at the office.

Mrs Gibbs at reception popped her head round the partition, "You alright? Where are you going?"

"I'm leaving." I threw the doors open and walked outside. The air was a shock to my lungs; it felt like I was breathing for the first time in weeks.

I took a shortcut through the park, wanting to get home to my unopened exam results, so I could check Miss Rowan hadn't got it wrong. The importance of my results had lost significance without Abby there to open them with me. They lay buried in a drawer.

A couple of girls were sitting smoking under one of the big oak trees, both wearing trilby hats, and it took me a moment to realise it was Abby's friends.

"Kat." Lisa waved and motioned for me to come over.

I walked towards them slowly, my chest tightening at the prospect of having to make small talk.

"How are you?" Lisa jumped up and hugged me awkwardly. My eyes met Chloe's over her shoulder. Chloe held my gaze briefly then looked away, taking a long drag of her cigarette.

I shrugged. "Okay. How are you doing?"

"We couldn't face school today. It's just not the same anymore, you know?" Lisa tapped some ash on the ground.

I nodded. Lisa and Chloe and a few others in my year had also been fairly friendly with the other four suicides and the pain of losing parts of a group of friends they'd had all their life was evident on their faces. I studied them both, searching for other signs of emotion in their expressions. For something like guilt...or a knowing. I'd spent the week after Abby's death phoning round all of her close friends demanding answers. Barely any of them could talk much through tears but they all said much the same: *"We just can't believe she would do this. She always seemed so happy."*

"You should come out with us at the weekend," Lisa said.

I looked at her in surprise. Chloe did too.

"Maybe, thanks." I never felt like I had much in common with Abby's friends – they were all obsessed with fashion and boys. I knew they called me her weird 'Emo' sister, having no clue as to what that actually meant. I hated being categorised; I was me, with my own style. Abby used to accuse me of treating them with disdain.

"We usually head down to this place called The Barn." Lisa said.

Chloe nudged her, wide-eyed.

"Where's that?" I asked.

"It's a disused warehouse place across the loch through Eddison Woods. Some art students from the city have refurbished it and use it as studio space. They let us hang out there at the weekends."

Eddison Woods. Where I found Abby, hanging from a tree. I shivered. "Did Abby go there?"

They exchanged looks and Chloe folded her arms, looking away.

"Yeah," Lisa said.

"Do the police know this?" I asked.

Lisa half shrugged, her eyes shifting back to Chloe.

Chloe stood up, pushing her hat back so I could see her eyes properly. Chloe had a luminous beauty and a cold exterior. There was something in her manner that accentuated this to the extreme. "They've visited but they don't know we hang about there. We don't want the police trying to shut the place down."

"Why would they do that?" I asked.

"Why d'you think? There's usually alcohol around...and drugs," she said. "Nothing major, and Abby never touched any drugs before you ask. The art students are into that scene. She must have written about it in her journal anyway and you have that now, right?"

I pursed my lips. "We've never found her journal. I've ripped her room apart, well as much as Mum and Dad will let me, and it's not there."

"Weird," Lisa frowned. "She used to take that thing around with her everywhere."

I turned back to Chloe. "Who else goes to this place?"

"Loads of people. People from our school, from other schools, uni students. It's about time we had some form of entertainment in this god-awful town," she huffed. "So don't go kicking up a fuss about it with the police. It's about the only thing keeping us all together right now."

I didn't say anything. They both sat back down, lighting fresh cigarettes.

"I've got to go." I looked at Lisa. "I'll maybe give you a call sometime."

"Sure." She gave me a small smile. "Take care of yourself, Kat."

I waved and walked on, wanting to know more about this Barn place. I wondered why Abby had never mentioned it to me.

I was relieved to find the drive empty when I arrived home. It meant that Mum had made it into work and had managed to stay there. She still had a distracted, empty look in her eyes. It made me feel nauseous. I desperately wanted comfort from her but she kept closing me out. I wondered if it was because she couldn't bear to look at me, to see Abby in my eyes. I had been applying my eyeliner even darker than usual, trying to take away the similarity, so that I too could look in the mirror without flinching. I dumped my bag in the hall and ran upstairs to my room, heading straight to the drawer where I'd hidden our exam results. I pulled out my envelope first, my hands shaking as I tore it open, even although I now knew what it was going to reveal. I scanned down the certificate: English – A, Maths – A, Modern Studies – A, French – A, History – A. Relief washed over me and I felt a glimmer of happiness. I immediately buried the emotion as I turned to look at Abby's unopened envelope.

Mum and Dad hadn't even remembered about the results. The day they had arrived hadn't been one of Mum's best. I didn't want her to be more upset, seeing an envelope addressed to Abby that she would never be able to open. Seeing results for exams that Abbey had worked so hard for, that now had no meaning.

I tore the envelope open and slid out the certificate. I scanned down the results. I re-read them, checking that it was definitely Abby's name written along the top. English – C, Spanish – D, Geography – D, Maths – D, Art – B. Abby had been on track for results similar to mine. Tears were hot behind my eyes.

Something had been very wrong and I never knew.

CHAPTER 2

I lay in bed listening to the sounds of Mum and Dad moving around. I wondered how long it would take Mum to notice that I hadn't got up yet. Maybe it wouldn't register.

Abby's results still spun round my head, guilt gnawing at my conscience. She'd always joked I was her 'big sister' as I was born first, by eight minutes. Growing up I was always fiercely protective of her and now when she'd needed me most I'd let her down.

"Hey, big sis."

I closed my eyes, replaying a recent conversation, the memory still so vivid I could picture Abby's face in clear detail.

"Hey." I looked up from my books and cleared a space on my bed so Abby could sit across from me. "What time is it?"

"One." Abby fiddled with her bracelet, a sign that she was either bored or wanted to talk.

I yawned, noticing she was wearing more make-up than usual. "Were you out tonight?"

She nodded, undoing clips from her hair so that her blonde curls tumbled around her shoulders.

"Where were you?"

"Just out with Chloe and Lisa." She reached forward and touched my knee, surprising me. "Hey, Kat. Remember when we used to tell each other everything?"

I smiled. "Sure. And speak in twin code?"

"Uggie, uggie." We laughed, the words sounding even more ridiculous now.

"Do you ever miss that?" She asked quietly.

I hesitated, thinking about the night I dyed my hair black, how desperate I was to forge a separate identify from her. "Sometimes."

"I do. Sometimes it feels like..." Her voice trailed off.

I looked back down at my books, a part of me knowing I should prompt her to finish the rest of her sentence as she clearly wanted to talk. But I was nearly finished cramming History, thirty more minutes then I could shut my eyes and curl up in bed.

"Hey, we should totally have a midnight feast, even although it's nearly one fifteen..." Her face lit up, eyes full of mischief.

I smiled halfheartedly. "I already stuffed my face with chocolate to keep awake. Let's do it after the exams, like as a celebration?"

"Oh, okay." She nodded. She lunged forward and gripped me in a hug. "Night, big sis."

A knock on my door interrupted my thoughts. "Kat, it's late. You'd better get up." It was Dad.

I jumped out of bed and opened my door. "I'm not going to school."

He looked at me. "Are you feeling alright?" His face tensed around the question as if he was scared of the answer.

"Yeah, it's not that... I found out yesterday that I got five As."

He looked at me blankly, taking a moment to understand what I was talking about.

"Your exams?" Recognition dawned on his face. A light appeared behind his eyes. "You got five As?"

I nodded, managing a small smile.

He smiled back. "Oh, Kat. That is so great." He hugged me and the contact overwhelmed me. I started to cry. I felt his arms tense around me. He patted me on the head and I pulled away, wiping at my tears.

"I'm sorry we forgot," he said.

I shook my head, wanting to tell him it was okay but I couldn't speak.

"I never saw them come in," he said.

"I took them and put them in my drawer." I looked up at him. "Dad, I opened Abby's too."

"Oh, well that's okay," he said.

"It's weird though, they weren't good..."

His face tensed. "We should talk about this later..."

"But don't you think it's strange? She always said she was studying. She must have been struggling and we didn't know..."

He shook his head. He looked so tired and lost. "I can't think about this just now, Kat. I have to go to work."

"I should let Mum know."

"No," he said firmly. "Just leave it."

I opened my mouth then closed it again. I wrapped my arms around my middle, feeling shivery.

"I'll talk to you later. You should go to school."

"No." I shook my head and he looked surprised. "I'm not going back. I don't need to."

"Well, you have to do something..."

"I'll get a job, save money and apply to uni next year." I braced myself, waiting for a challenge.

He sighed. "Okay. Just make sure you get started on looking today."

"Fine." I nodded. "See you later." I walked back into my room and shut the door. I lay down on my bed, looking around at the posters circling the walls. My parents had analysed them and asked me about my music, my books. The images of vampires, Marilyn Manson, gothic-looking figures from horror films...

Mum had cornered me in my room one evening.

"Did she like the same music as you? Marilyn Manson? Did she listen to this too?"

I looked at her. "Have you seen her room?"

"Don't be smart, Kat. I'm just asking..."

"She hated Marilyn Manson; she said he was the spawn of the devil. She hated all of my music, she hated vampires and you know she hated my make-up and my clothes. And I'm not in any satanic cult and I didn't recruit Abby to anything like it, in case that was

your next question."

Mum pursed her lips. "Did you notice anything unusual about Abby's behaviour?"

Did I? I kept replaying images of those weeks, months before her death, over and over in my head. What she had said, times we had spent together. She just seemed like Abby.

"She was hardly in over the holidays when you were at work," I said. "But that wasn't unusual. You know...she had...a lot of friends. "

"What about boyfriends? She stopped talking to me about boys."

I pictured Gordon, the way he followed her around like a sick puppy last year and how Abby had given in and gone on a few dates. "Just that guy, Gordon Hamill, remember? But that didn't last long."

Recognition dawned on Mum's face. "That's right, he's a nice boy. He seemed really fond of Abby. She didn't seem upset when they split up... Was she?"

I shook my head. "Abby wasn't really that into him. I think she felt sorry for him more than anything."

"Anyone else? Maybe older boys?"

"Not that I know of." I realised that I hadn't really shared much about boys with Abby. She used to try to talk to me about it but must have given up when I rolled my eyes at the mention of every loser she picked out at school as her latest crush.

"Do you have a boyfriend?" Mum asked me.

I frowned. "No." I wanted to know why that would be important. "Why aren't the police investigating more, Mum? This just wasn't like Abby."

Her face was sad and drawn. "They said the procurator fiscal ruled out any suspicious circumstances and no links have been found between the suicides. I know it's difficult, Kat..."

I closed my eyes and climbed back into bed, pulling the covers up over my head. Difficult didn't come close.

The sound of the coffee machine whooshing and the smell of apple pie hit me as soon as I walked through the door of Cake Tin; instant comfort. I walked up to the counter, watching the boy serving. I hadn't seen him before. He was tall, with floppy dark hair, and was wearing a faded checked shirt with the sleeves rolled up. I slid up onto a stool at the counter and waited for him to notice me. I pulled my CV out of my bag and re-read it, hoping it didn't sound too pathetic. I'd only ever done some weekend work in a local petrol station and that had only lasted for a couple of months.

"Hi, what can I get you?"

I looked up into his smiling face. His eyes were a pale blue.

"Hi. I'd like a job please." I handed him my CV. "And a hot chocolate would also be nice."

He took my CV. "I'm not sure a job is on the menu today. Let me just check for you..." He started to read down my CV and wandered through the back.

I strained forward on my stool, trying to see what he was doing. I could see he was talking to someone in the kitchen.

A minute later Mrs Hodge walked out. She smiled when she saw me. "Oh, it's Kat Sullivan. Hi, sweetheart."

"Hi." I gave her a little wave. "Don't suppose you're looking for staff?"

"We are struggling a bit since James went off to university. But shouldn't you be at school?"

"I'm not going back for a sixth year. I want to save some money for uni next year."

She nodded. Her eyes were full of concern and I looked away.

"Are your parents okay with that?"

I shrugged. "I guess so."

"And how are you all?" she asked.

"We're okay." Just slowly falling apart at the seams.

Checked-shirt boy appeared with a hot chocolate. He laid extra marshmallows at the side of the plate. I smiled a thank you.

"Did she get the job?" he asked Mrs Hodge.

She studied me, like she was weighing things up in her mind. "You got cash-handling and till experience in the petrol station?"

I nodded enthusiastically. "I picked it up really quickly too."

"I think we should start you off on a trial basis first. How's about you give Kat a quick training session once she's finished her hot chocolate? Would that be alright doing a short shift this afternoon, Kat? We're quiet on a Tuesday so you'll get time to find your feet."

"That would be great. Thanks."

Mrs Hodge winked at me then walked back through to the kitchen.

Checked-shirt boy held out his hand and I shook it, hoping he didn't notice that my palm was a bit sweaty.

"I'm Callum."

"Kat." I stirred the cream into my hot chocolate. "I've not seen you around here before."

"We just moved here over the summer."

"You at uni?"

He nodded. "Just started last week at Riverside University in the City. I'm studying English and Philosophy. "

"And how's that working out?"

"Good," he smiled. "So far, so fascinating. How about you? Did I hear you say you left school?"

"Yeah," I said. "You got any brothers or sisters at the school?"

"A younger brother, Tom. He just started fifth year at Eddison High. How about you?"

The question caught me off guard, even though I should have expected it. I was so used to being part of a small town where everyone knew everyone else and their business. I glanced at the newspaper sitting folded up at the end of the counter. I reached across and picked it up, flicking through the pages. I stopped at page five and turned the paper around, so that Callum could see.

"That's my sister, Abby." I tapped the photograph under the heading 'Scottish Suicide Town.'

Callum glanced at the story then back at me. "I'm sorry. I thought you looked familiar when you came in, but I didn't make the connection."

I pulled apart one of my marshmallows, trying to distract myself from the tight feeling forming in my throat. It would be beyond embarrassing breaking down in front of Callum.

"My parents were a bit hesitant about moving here, because of everything. It seems like an okay town so far, though there's not much to do is there?" he said.

"It's a pretty boring place." I shrugged. "Though some girls told me that there's this place everyone has started going to called the Barn."

"Yeah, Tom mentioned it."

I looked at him curiously, wondering how his brother, who had been here five minutes, had heard about this place and I hadn't.

"It sounds a bit weird to me. Some art students trying to reconstruct something from the Sixties."

"What d'you mean?" I frowned.

"From Tom's description of the decor and the kind of vibe of the place it sounds like they want it to be like Andy Warhol's Factory, his studio where weird arty and druggy people congregated."

"Andy Warhol... that artist who did the Campbell soup can paintings?"

Callum nodded. "Yeah, he was totally nuts. He used to make weird underground porno type films too."

"You don't think they're going to copy that too?" I raised my eyebrows at him.

He laughed. "I doubt it. I don't think Tom would have been up for that kind of thing."

I watched as Callum poured himself a glass of milk. There was something about his manner which put me at ease. I realised this was the first conversation I'd had in ages that didn't feel strained or pitying. "You know, it's kind of nice talking to someone who doesn't really know me," I said. "So can we make a deal?"

"Sure, what?"

"Don't give me any special treatment okay?"

"Alright. No special treatment." he smiled. "You do realise that means I'm going to work you extra hard this afternoon?"

I drained the remainders of my hot chocolate. "Bring it on!" I slid down off the stool and walked round to join him behind the counter, hoping I looked a lot more confident than I felt.

"Give me your bag and I'll take it through the back for you."

I slid my bag up over my head and he took it from me, disappearing back through the kitchen.

I stood looking out at the cafe. It looked different from this side of the counter. The buttons were labelled with the names of foods and drinks. I hoped that meant it would automatically input the prices of items, which might make remembering things a bit easier.

The bell on the door chimed, signalling the arrival of a new customer. I glanced at the kitchen door, my heart hammering, willing Callum to hurry up and come back. Smoothing my top, I stood up straighter, hoping I looked self-assured and professional.

A boy a few years older than me wandered in. He turned to hold the door open for two of his friends, deep in conversation with one of them. My eyes were drawn to the one at the back. He wasn't talking and hung back slightly, taking in his surroundings. He had messy dark hair, with streaks of blonde running through it. His cheekbones were so sculpted they almost cast shadows on his face and his eyes looked black.

I knew I was staring but there was something about him that made it impossible not to. I realised his friends were looking at me and I flushed. They stopped talking, a look of confusion on their faces.

He shot them a questioning glance then followed their gaze towards me. He stared at me and I looked back. The colour drained from his face. I opened my mouth to say something, to ask him what was wrong. He shook his head, turned and walked back out the door. His friends quickly followed.

"Wait!" I shouted. I started to move from behind the counter. Callum appeared, grabbing my arm.

"What is it?" he asked me. "Do you know them?"

I shook my head, feeling dizzy with confusion. "No, I've never seen them before... The way that guy looked at me, as if he'd seen a ghost. I think he thought I was Abby." The image of the shock in his eyes flashed in front of me. Who was he, and how did he know my sister?

CHAPTER 3

When I switched my mobile on I had three voicemail messages from Sarah and some texts from other friends asking me where I was, why I hadn't been back at school. Sarah sounded uncomfortable in her messages, saying in a quiet voice that she 'hoped I was okay'. I could tell her I wasn't okay, but I felt she shouldn't have to ask, that she should know and just be here for me, no questions asked. I wanted her to try harder. I wanted her to be my friend again.

I scrolled down through my contacts and stopped at Lisa's name. I pressed dial and the phone rang a couple of beats before she came on the line.

"Hi Kat. How's things?"

"Okay." I glanced at my reflection in the mirror and rubbed my lips together, my burgundy lipstick bleeding into the cracks. "Are you still going out this weekend, to that place, the Barn?"

"Yeah. We were thinking of going tonight. You want to come?"

I hesitated, not wanting to arrive alone, but the thought of having to walk through Eddison Woods to get there was something I knew I wasn't ready for. "I want to come, but I'll just find you there later, if you tell me where it is." I scribbled down directions and slid the notebook into my bag.

I turned back to the mirror and pinned my hair up. I dipped a finger into my black eye shadow pot, applying an extra coat. The shards of glitter in the powder shimmered under the light. I scrutinised the rest of my reflection, wondering if the black corset with jeans was too dressy. Or maybe not dressy enough? I wish I'd thought to ask Lisa. My palms were sweating at the prospect of having to hang around with a large group of people I barely knew, but I needed to see this place for myself, hopefully find out more about Abby's life there.

I glanced at the clock on my bedside table. Eight. I decided to wait an hour before leaving. The image of the guy from earlier in the week was still imprinted on my brain. I hoped Lisa and Chloe would maybe be able to tell me who he was. Or maybe something else could...

Reaching under my bed I pulled out my laptop. I flipped it open and clicked on the browser. As the icon swirled into action I looked at my phone, debating about inviting Sarah to come with me tonight. She didn't really like Abby's friends, they didn't really like her. I wanted them to talk to me properly, maybe give me some insights into what Abby had been like with them. I doubted they would be open with Sarah around.

I turned back to my laptop and logged onto Abby's tribute page. I swallowed the feeling of nausea that trailed up my body as I clicked. I had wanted to delete it, screaming at my parents to let me, that it was sick. Mum, on seeing that Abby's friends had created it, wouldn't let me. She said it was what Abby would have wanted, having a place where her friends could leave her messages. I think really it was what Mum wanted. I suspected she logged on regularly, seeking comfort in the gushing accolades posted on the wall.

I avoided looking at Abby's photo as the page popped up. It took me a few seconds to notice that the members of the page had increased to 2,000.

I scrolled down the list of people, looking for names or faces that I recognised. Who were these people? Why did they care about my sister, a person they had never met? I realised I'd never be able to find his picture in amongst this. I needed to know his name at least before I could search properly.

I hesitated, then began to read some recent postings left on the wall.

'May the angels in heaven look after you now. God bless.' From some woman named Martha.

'We miss your beautiful face every day in school, RIP babes xx.' Written by a girl she barely knew from the year below us.

I slammed the lid of my laptop down. They had no right. I shoved my laptop back under the bed, banging it against my metal storage box of CDs. I picked up one of my boots and threw it across the room, wanting to break something but instead knocking down a row of books. I braced myself, waiting for Mum or Dad to come rushing in. Neither did.

They would be in the Conservatory, watching TV and drinking wine. It had become their evening ritual. Mum had stopped going to her martial arts classes. Dad had stopped going down the local pub. I suspected they couldn't handle the questions, the well wishers and looks of pity. They could barely even talk to me, let alone anyone else in the town.

We'd had a lot of visitors in the first few weeks, bringing us meals, flowers, words of comfort. Then their visits became less frequent and gradually stopped; the discomfort of one-sided conversation and debilitating grief fending off even the most determined of friends.

I opened my door and looked across the hallway to Abby's old room. I had only been in once to look for her journal. I knew Dad had got rid of a lot of her stuff, giving her clothes to charity, to friends. He had offered me some but I refused to even look at them. We never liked the same things anyway; not for years. An image of us dressed identically, giggling under Abby's covers as we devoured a midnight feast of birthday cake and sweets, flashed through my head. That was the day we'd got away with swapping places at a friend's eleventh birthday party, one of our finest moments.

My hand shook as I turned the handle. The door creaked loudly, like the hinges were starting to rust now that the room lay empty.

A stream of light from outside illuminated parts of the room; the bed, her dressing table. I walked over to the dresser and ran my hand over her jewellery box. I clicked it open and looked inside. It was stuffed full of her necklaces, rings, earrings and bracelets. I wondered why Dad had left them.

I pulled out a silver charm bracelet and held it up to the light, the row of crescent moons and stars swinging from side to side. I slid it up onto my wrist, a perfect fit of course. I fingered one of the stars, imagining Abby was somewhere out there, watching me.

Or maybe a part of her still lay inside these charms and if I kept them close to me she would be with me, always. The thought was comforting.

Glancing around the room I noticed a painting propped up beside her bed, facing the wrong way round. Why had I never noticed that before? I walked over and crouched down to turn it around. I switched on the bedside lamp and was taken aback when I realised it was a portrait of Abby. It wasn't an obvious likeness as it was done in a kind of abstract, wild style. Her face was side on and her hair was a mane of gold and orange and brown waves, her eyes closed, dark lashes curling against her golden skin, but I knew it was her. I ran a finger along her cheek, the paint thick beneath my touch.

A signature was scrawled in the bottom corner; I squinted to make it out. Rod? No, Rob. I ran the name over in my mind, trying to remember if Abby had ever mentioned him. I couldn't think. I'd ask Lisa and Chloe if they knew him.

I switched off the light and carried the painting into my room. I wondered if Mum and Dad had noticed it. Something niggled inside of me, telling me that there was something important about this.

I came to a crossroads at the path and looked to the left, then to the right. It was too dark to read the directions I'd scribbled down and I realised with a sinking feeling that I was lost. Looking up ahead, I tilted my head to the side, hearing a *thump, thump... thump.* Music. I followed the thumps, which soon developed into a rhythmic melody. Lights shone through the trees and I strained to see the outline of a large building in the distance. That had to be it.

I half ran the rest of the way, my breath coming out in short gasps, more from nerves than exhaustion. I swallowed and looked up at the 'barn'. The windows were high but I could make out lights flashing from inside, and shadows moving against the walls. I'd never even stepped inside a pub, never mind somewhere like this... My stomach flipped with nerves and I had to fight an overwhelming sensation to run back home.

"Keep going, do this for Abby," I whispered to myself.

There was no distinct entrance. I walked around the side and found what looked like a door. I tried the handle. It didn't budge. The music was loud, the walls outside throbbing in time with the beats. I knocked on the door. Nothing. I tightened my hand into a fist and pounded hard.

The door creaked open a gap.

"Yes?" An eye and half a mouth peeked through the slit.

"Oh, hi. Is this...the Barn?"

"Who wants to know?" the voice asked. The door opened a bit wider to reveal a girl with spiky red hair.

"I'm Kat. I'm from...Eddison High. Well, I used to go there..." My toes curled inside my boots. *Lame. Totally lame.*

"Are you here alone?" the girl asked, peering over my shoulder into the night.

"Yes." I nodded. "I'm meeting friends here. Lisa and Chloe."

I held my breath as the girl slowly looked me up and down.

"Enter." The door swung open to reveal that she was perched on top of a stool, a tin box hanging around her neck. "We ask for a little donation. As much as you want to give."

"Oh, sure," I reached into my bag, feeling around for my purse, my hands shaking slightly. My eyes were drawn to the girl's stripy tights and purple feathered skirt. No need for me to worry about being overdressed. I pulled out a few coins, dropping them into the tin.

"We appreciate your love." She flashed me a grin, her lips a dark red. "Enjoy your time here."

I turned to look at the staircase behind her, the sounds of music and voices floating down. Taking a deep breath I climbed the stairs, my heart beating faster with every step. On the walls at either side of the stairs hung STRICTLY NO PHOTOGRAPHY signs, with a smaller print underneath saying, 'You and your camera/phone will be thrown out and banned forevermore.'

As I stepped up into the open space my senses were overloaded with the scene before me. The walls shone silver and black, some sides left with natural brick showing. Large paintings were dotted around, a mixture of half-painted images, one canvas with explosions of colour, as if someone had picked up pots of paint and thrown them against the surface. Images of Marilyn Monroe, James Dean, Kurt Cobain and Coca Cola bottles were pasted on pillars around the room. Sofas and antique-looking chairs were dotted around randomly. Groups of older teenagers sat bunched together on sofas and some sat cross-legged on rugs on the floor. I walked into the space, noticing that sections of the room were cordoned off with white sheets; easels and paints peeking out from behind the drapes.

Turning a corner, I was startled to see a video projection against the back wall, black and white stills of people, flashing in time with the music playing. To the right of the video was a piano. An old man dressed in a long coat and hat sat at the piano, running his hands up and down the keys but not actually pressing down on any of them. It felt like I had stepped into a weird, psychedelic dream.

"Evening."

I blinked, the voice breaking the spell of wonder that the place had cast upon me. I turned around to see a boy holding up a bottle of vodka.

"You want a drink?" he asked. He looked down at my empty hands. "You're supposed to bring your own bottle but I don't mind if you share mine."

I shook my head, making a face. "Thanks, but I don't like vodka."

"Maybe you'd prefer a beer?" Another male stepped in beside us. He held out a brand of beer I'd never heard of. I took it from him, sensing something familiar about his face.

"What's your name?" he asked.

The boy looked at him, then me, shrugged, and walked off.

"Kat."

"I'm Michael." He shook my hand. "You work at Cake Tin, don't you?"

"Yeah," I nodded, taking a sip of the beer. It tasted sour with a little kick of sweetness. I frowned. "Did I serve you there this week?"

"Serve me?" he smirked. "I like the sound of that."

My face flushed. I took another swig of beer; this time it was more of a gulp.

"We left before you got the chance," he said.

We. I looked at him again, this time remembering. He had been one of the friends...of *that guy*. "I remember. Your friend...the guy with the blonde streaks...he looked pretty shocked when he saw me. Did you know my sister?"

"You have a sister?" His beer bottle hovered against his lips; his eyes were teasing, like he was playing with me.

Irritation flared in my gut. "I did have a sister, a twin. Her name was Abby."

"Kat!"

I stumbled as arms were thrown around my neck and I was hit with an overwhelming cloud of perfume. I turned to see Lisa and Chloe.

"Well, well. If it isn't the flower girls. How are we tonight, ladies?" Michael raised an eyebrow at them.

Lisa giggled into her glass of wine. "Fantastic. As always." She clinked her glass against Chloe's. Chloe wasn't paying attention; her eyes searching the room as though looking for someone. Both of them had flowers in their hair and were wearing floaty skirts and lacy tops. I felt out of place beside them.

"Isn't this place fantastic?" Lisa gushed in my ear. Her breath smelled of wine and bubble gum.

I nodded. "It's pretty 'out there'." I turned back to Michael. "You never answered my question."

"I talked to your sister a couple of times," he said. He looked me up and down. "You don't look that much like her."

"Did your friend know her too?" I asked.

He hesitated, as though he was trying to suss me out. He shrugged. "He talked to her a few times."

"Is Rob here?" Chloe moved forward, side-stepping Lisa who was spinning around to the music.

The signature on the painting I'd found in Abby's room flashed into my head. "Who's Rob?" I turned to Chloe, then to Michael.

Michael chuckled softly into his beer bottle. "He's around here somewhere. If I see him I'll let him know you were looking for him."

Chloe tossed her hair behind her shoulder, giving a little nonchalant shrug. "Don't bother. I'll catch up with him whenever."

Michael turned to me and nodded his head. "Catch you later, Kitty Kat."

I watched him disappear into the crowds then turned back to Chloe. "Who's Rob?"

She avoided eye contact. "One of Michael's friends."

"He's one of the art students who put this place together." Lisa said. She giggled. "Chloe lurvvves him."

"No I don't." Chloe glared at her.

Lisa rolled her eyes, nodding her head at me.

"What does he look like?" I asked.

"Drop dead gorgeous," Lisa said, licking her lips. Her eyes widened. "I mean gorgeous, you know."

I frowned, wondering why she looked panicked. Then I realised she had spoken a word which could not be spoken around me. *Dead, death.* There was a code of silence in place that dictated certain topics of conversation should be avoided.

"Why do you want to know what he looks like?" Chloe asked.

I shrugged. "I think I might have seen him the other day." I didn't feel like telling either of them about the painting. I took another sip of beer and scanned the crowds, looked back at the video playing on the wall. This place was so weird, but great. I was hurt that Abby had never invited me. Probably thought I wasn't cool enough.

"I believe you've been looking for me?"

I noticed the startled look on Chloe's face, the way her cheeks flushed and how her body kicked into preening mode. I knew before I turned around that the voice belonged to Rob.

He stepped forward and walked round to face me. He only glanced at Chloe and I wondered if he'd addressed the question to her or to me. His eyes were just as black as they had looked from a distance in the café and he had that pull, that something that prevented me from looking away, even although I wanted to. It felt like he was analysing every inch of me and it unnerved me. I wanted to walk away.

"You're Abby's sister?" he said. His voice was soft, barely a whisper.

I nodded. I couldn't find my voice to speak.

CHAPTER 4

It felt like forever, the two of us standing there, just staring at each other. I looked away first.

Chloe threw me a look of hatred before turning her attention to him. She touched him on the arm and I knew his eyes were still on me. I began to feel embarrassed. I was never comfortable with attention and this was really testing my limits.

"Are you playing tonight, Rob?" Chloe asked him.

He took a moment to answer. "Later."

I turned away from them, draining the remainder of my beer, looking for somewhere to put the empty bottle. "Be right back," I said to Lisa. I hurried through the crowds, side-stepping the elbows and feet of those dancing. A hand touched my arm. My heart jumped.

"Why are you running away?"

I stopped and turned to look at him. He loomed above me; it made me feel small and fragile looking up at him even although I was at least five foot seven in my boots. "I'm not running away."

He looked me up and down. "You never told me your name."

I folded my arms. "You didn't ask."

"You never gave me the opportunity." He held out his hand. "I'm Rob."

I hesitated then slid my hand into his. His skin felt warm, his fingers slender. He held onto my hand a little longer than necessary.

"Kat."

He scratched the stubble above a cleft on his chin. "I used to have a cat called cat."

"How imaginative. I bet you didn't spell it with a K."

He looked at me, his eyes narrowing slightly, like he was

processing something in his head. "No."

I glanced around the room. "I heard that you were responsible for putting this place together."

He tore his eyes away from me and followed my gaze around the room. "I had some help. What do you think? You like it?"

I nodded. "It's different."

His mouth curled into a half smile. "Certainly is." I was aware of him scrutinising my face again. "You look so much like Abby."

Hearing him speak her name unnerved me. "Well, we were identical twins."

"Your eyes…that amazing shade of pale green. Your eyeliner makes it stand out even more." He paused. "You have different mannerisms though. You're more…closed."

"Abby could be too open sometimes."

"Oh yeah?" he said.

"Yeah," I said.

"Does it make you uncomfortable me talking about your sister? Should I stop?"

There was something about his unapologetic manner – the way that he wasn't scared to talk about her – that was so refreshing.

"Did you know her well?" I asked.

His face didn't give away any emotion.

"In a sense," he said.

"In a sense?" I prompted him for an explanation.

"Well, how well do we really know anyone?" he said. He glanced down at my wrist, the one where Abby's charm bracelet hung; stars and moons twinkling under the lights. His eyes bore into mine. "How well do you think you knew your sister?"

Having someone else ask the question unsettled me, more so than when it circled around my head. I wasn't sure I wanted to face the answer. "I'm beginning to think probably not as well as I thought I did."

He didn't say anything. There was no apology or pity in his eyes.

A girl appeared beside us, smiling and laughing. She swayed her hips flirtatiously and ran a hand slowly up Rob's arm, dancing close beside him, trailing a scarf around his neck. He stood and let her, not showing much reaction, simply glancing at her before returning to look at me. He made me feel like I was the only person in the room. Never before had anyone offered me such uninterrupted attention, especially not a male. The girl eventually moved on, realising that she wasn't going to entice him to dance with her.

"I found a painting of my sister earlier. I think you might have done it," I said.

Something sparked behind his eyes. "I like to paint people who come here. I've done a couple of Abby. What did you think?"

"It was kind of abstract," I said.

"Just like your sister." His lips formed that half smile again.

"What do you mean?"

"She was hard to define..."

I had never thought of Abby as being a complex person. Her emotions were always clearly accessible, she was open, friendly – he had just said himself that she was more open than me.

"She was full of contradictions," he elaborated, but it didn't clarify anything.

"Rob, we're on in ten." Michael appeared, placing a hand on his shoulder. He glanced at me.

Rob nodded in acknowledgement. He turned back to me. "Are you planning on staying on for a bit?"

I nodded.

"I'll catch you after my set. In fact..." He shrugged out of his leather jacket. "D'you mind holding on to this for me? I don't like leaving it lying around...things sometimes go missing around here."

"Oh." I took the jacket. It was heavy in my arms and smelled of a musky aftershave that made my toes tingle. "You're in a band?"

"Yeah," he said and then disappeared into the crowd. I watched his retreating back; his arms had a lean muscle and I caught a flash of tattooed words running down the lower side of one of them. I wondered how old he was. Nineteen? Maybe twenty.

I walked into the crowd and watched curtains being pulled open up ahead to reveal a little stage area, with a drum kit set up and a stack of amps at the back. A large mirror hung behind the stage and a girl lit candles, which sat in tall stands at either side of the area.

Michael walked onto the stage first, followed by one of the other guys who had been in the cafe with them. They both bent down to pick up guitars. A boy with long blonde hair sat down behind the drums and then Rob walked across the stage. The music that had been playing throughout the evening silenced and people stopped dancing, turning to face the stage. Rob stood in its centre, reaching to adjust a microphone. Someone wolf-whistled from the crowd but he didn't react. Michael slung a guitar over his shoulder and Rob picked up one at his feet, turning his back on the crowd.

Michael stepped towards a microphone. "Evening."

A whoop circled the room and people cheered.

"Thanks for joining us tonight."

The lights dimmed and the music started, guitars in minor key, the drums playing a stuttering beat. Rob turned around to face the crowd and his voice filled the air, haunting and intense. My heart kicked against my chest.

Girls beside me were throwing their bodies around in time to the music, their eyes never leaving the stage. I stepped away from them, watching him as he sang and played. His fingers strummed the guitar frantically, his body moved in time with the music, a passion radiating from him. The music was loud and dark and raw. Something stirred inside my soul. I gripped his jacket tighter, his scent surrounding me.

There was a break in the riff and he looked up, his eyes scanning the crowd as he sang quieter, whispering almost. I wasn't paying attention to the words. I felt like I was being pulled in, closer towards the stage. He looked in my direction just as the music picked up tempo. I looked back. The music pulsated through the soles of my feet, winding up to create butterflies in my abdomen. He was dangerously attractive. *Look away, look away. Don't let him see that you're hypnotised by his performance.* My inner voice wasn't strong enough to penetrate the spell.

Someone tapped my shoulder. I didn't react, not wanting to look away from the stage.

"Kat." A familiar voice shouted in my ear.

I blinked and looked up to see Callum. "Oh, hi."

"Hi." He looked over to the stage frowning. "Who are they?"

"Just some guys…" I noticed a boy standing a bit behind Callum, arms folded, a sulky expression on his face.

"That's Relapse," the boy said in a tone that implied everyone knew that.

Callum raised his eyebrows at me. "This is my brother, Tom."

"Oh." I looked at the boy again, now seeing the similarity beneath the longer fairer hair and faint eyeliner. "Hi."

Tom offered me a half wave.

"What are you doing here?" Callum said.

I shrugged. "I wanted to see what it was like. How about you? You hadn't sounded too enthralled about the place."

Callum made a face. "My parents sent me to find him." He nodded at Tom. "He's apparently grounded for coming home drunk and disorderly the other night so shouldn't be out."

"Can we just go?" Tom said.

"You want a lift home?" Callum asked me.

I looked back at the stage; saw Rob thrashing out another tune on his guitar. I looked down at his jacket. "I said I'd hold onto this… until after the set…" I nodded towards the band.

"Oh, right," Callum said.

I felt that draw again, like the music was pulling me in. My head began to spin. I turned back to Callum, suddenly liking the idea of leaving and getting back home. "If you hang on a minute I'll find someone to leave it with."

"Okay, sure," he smiled. Tom sighed loudly. Callum turned to him and smacked him playfully on the forehead. Tom pushed at his hand, frantically smoothing back the hair he had messed up.

The crowd was becoming more rowdy, people were jumping up and down and waving their arms around and I had to duck and weave in and out of bodies to avoid being punched in the nose. A hand circled my wrist and I stopped, startled to see my friend Jill.

"Kat, how are you? I never thought I'd see you here. Why haven't you been back at school?"

I looked into her questioning eyes; saw the traces of concern and pity.

"I decided I didn't want to stay on," I said. "I want to save some money for uni."

"You got a job?"

I nodded. "I started at Cake Tin."

"Oh, cool. We'll come in and see you sometime." Jill smiled. "Sarah is worried about you."

A pang hit me somewhere deep inside. "I have to go. I'll see you later."

"Oh, okay. You take care, Kat."

Her hand brushed my arm and I walked away, looking for Lisa and Chloe. I finally spotted them standing on one of the sofas. I waved but they were oblivious to me. I tugged on Lisa's sleeve.

"Lisa," I called. She looked down at me and it took her a while to process who I was. She smiled a dreamy, drunken smile.

"Oh, hi Kat. Where've you been?" She didn't want an answer. She turned back to watch the band, shouting a whoop of approval.

Chloe hopped down off the sofa, looking at the jacket in my arms.

"Where did you get that?" she asked.

"Rob asked me to keep a hold of it for him."

Chloe's lips tightened into a straight line. She looked over to the stage then turned her attention back to me. "He does this you know."

"Does what?" I said.

"Has his flavour of the month. Then when he tastes you he gets bored and moves on."

"That sounds a bit…seedy," I said, wondering if she had been his flavour of the month, or maybe she was hoping she was going to be. "I was just holding his jacket for him. But I have to go, so could you take it, give it back to him after the set?"

Her face remained composed, but I could see a spark of excitement in her eyes. She took the jacket from me. "Sure."

"Thanks. Well, I'll see you later." I looked up at Lisa. "Bye Lisa."

I walked towards the back of the room, in the direction of the staircase where I could see Callum and Tom standing waiting for me. I turned back briefly and saw Chloe sliding her arms into Rob's jacket, pulling it close around her. Traces of his scent still clung to my skin and I knew she would be breathing him in. I looked back to the stage and Rob was scanning the crowd again. A part of me wondered if he was looking for me; a part of me hoped so.

Callum smiled as I approached. "Ready?"

I nodded. "Yeah, let's get out of here."

CHAPTER 5

Something dark curled inside of me the next day. My limbs felt heavy as I walked to work, as if weights were dragging at my legs and seeping into my bones. Bad thoughts circled my head, like whispers of sorrow. I buttoned my coat up all the way to the top and sunk my chin in under the collar. I avoided eye contact on the street, not wanting to talk to anyone. The sun hurt my eyes. I wanted it to go away.

I pushed open the door to Cake Tin. Callum was standing behind the counter, unloading the dishwasher. My heart sank; I had hoped I would be working a shift with Peter, a quiet boy who only talked if you asked him a direct question.

"Morning," Callum called as I walked past into the kitchen and through to the back to hang up my coat and bag. Mrs Hodge was stirring soup in the kitchen and held out a spoonful to me as I reappeared.

"Kat, you'll have better taste buds than me. What do you think, more salt?"

I took the spoon and the soup was hot on my tongue but to me it tasted of nothing. "A little." I laid the spoon down and opened the fridge, pulling down a beaker of salad dressing to fill up jars for lunchtime. The methodical motion of pouring the liquid into the jar soothed me. My mind emptied and the sense of doom began to lift from my shoulders. I wasn't sure what emotion was creeping around me but I didn't like it; I didn't want to return to that dark place I had visited in the weeks after Abby's death. I was supposed to be moving on from that.

"How's things?" Callum asked cheerfully, reaching down to pull out some Danish pastries to re-fill the cake tray.

"Okay," I said, focusing on pouring more salad dressing. I placed the filled jars back in the fridge and walked out to the serving area. I turned up the stereo, wanting to drown out my own thoughts.

"You okay?" Callum looked over at me.

"Fine," I said, watching the numbers ticking over as the music played.

I knew he wasn't convinced. He turned on the coffee machine. "Want a cappuccino?"

"No thanks."

"What did you think of the Barn?" he asked, frothing the milk, steam circling his arms.

A spark of excitement shot through me as I pictured the weird and wonderful set-up of the place, and thought back to the image of Rob singing... "It was...different. Much better than the cheesy clubs in the city, I imagine."

"Hmm," Callum looked thoughtful.

"What did you think?"

"I'm not sure. There was something a bit...off about the place. Did you notice how a lot of the pictures on the walls were of dead icons – ones who had committed suicide...sorry," He glanced at me, as if checking I wasn't going to burst into tears. "I just thought that was a bit tasteless, what with everything."

I recalled images of Marilyn Monroe, Kurt Cobain...popular cult stars. "I doubt that was intentional."

"I don't know; I left with a kind of strange feeling. There was something unsettling about that band. That singer guy – did you speak to him?"

"A bit." I looked at him. "Why d'you ask?"

Callum shrugged. "Tom talks about him a lot. Thinks he's the best thing since sliced bread. He's 'so cool, man'. I think I've heard him say that at least a dozen times the past few days."

"Yeah, well. I suppose he's going for that whole moody 'too cool for school' persona," I said.

"It's amazing how many people get sucked in with that garbage. Particularly females." He looked at me pointedly.

"You trying to say we're gullible?" I folded my arms.

"I'm sure there are some smart girls out there who can see it for what it is."

I turned away, wondering why he was so bothered by someone he barely even knew. "Was Tom in a lot of trouble with your parents?" I said, changing the subject.

Callum smirked. "Grounded for another month."

I raised an eyebrow. "Harsh. D'you reckon he'll last that long?"

"No chance. He'll find some way of escaping," he said. "He's turning into a bit of a rebel. Never thought Tom would be like that. I'm not sure if it's got something to do with moving to a new place. I think he might be trying a bit too hard to fit in."

I thought of how hard it must be, starting a new school at sixteen, especially in a small place like Eddison, where most people had known one another since birth. "Where did you move from?"

"A small town outside Edinburgh. We'd lived there all our lives so I think we're all finding it a bit difficult adjusting. Maybe not so much me; I was ready for change going to uni and all that."

"Wouldn't you rather live away from home?"

Callum shrugged. "I can't really afford it just now. I'm also not much of a party animal so the idea of living in halls doesn't really appeal to me."

I tried to picture myself living in close proximity with a bunch of students and realised the idea didn't really appeal to me either.

"Are you planning on going to university?" he asked.

"Yeah," I nodded. "Next year hopefully."

"Do you know what you want to study?"

"Law," I said.

He raised an eyebrow. "Tough course. Why d'you want to be a lawyer?"

I shrugged. "I hate injustice. And I like to win arguments."

"I can imagine." He smiled.

The door chimed and I looked up to see our first customers of the day. Jill and Sarah walked in, Sarah hanging back a bit, her steps hesitant. I sucked in my breath. Jill gave me a little wave. I returned the gesture with a small smile.

"Friends of yours?" Callum asked.

"Yeah," I said.

"Hey Kat," Jill called. She glanced at Callum, her smile widening.

"Hi." I directed my greeting at Sarah.

"Hi," she said. "How are you?"

"Okay," I replied, fiddling with the dishcloth that was behind the counter. "You?"

"Okay," she said.

"Can I get you ladies anything?" Callum came over.

"A mocha. With some marshmallows and cream please," Jill said. She stuck out her hand. "I'm Jill."

"Callum."

Sarah glanced around the cafe, unaware that Callum was waiting on her order.

Jill rolled her eyes and turned back to Callum. "She'll have the same."

"Okay, two mochas coming up." He turned to me, "Why don't you have a break, Kat? I'll bring you one too."

"I just got here," I said.

"It's quiet. Go and sit with your friends."

Thanks Callum.

Jill smiled at me eagerly. Sarah studied the paintings hanging on the walls.

I walked from behind the counter and led them over to a table in the corner of the cafe. Jill took the seat nearest me and Sarah sat across from me.

"It's so great that you're working here," Jill said. "I love it in here." She leaned in closer to me. "And Callum is a total hottie. Where's he from?"

"His family just moved here."

"I saw you leaving the Barn with him the other night. Are you going out?"

Sarah snapped to full attention at this question. She looked at me curiously.

"No, no," I shook my head. "He just offered me a lift home. He was picking up his wee brother."

"How did you hear about the Barn?" Sarah asked quietly.

I hesitated. "Lisa and Chloe told me about it. They said Abby used to hang around there."

"What was it like?" she asked.

"It's fantastic," Jill said. "We should all go together next weekend."

Sarah shook her head. "There's no way my Dad would let me go."

Jill snorted. "No one asks their parents if they can go. In fact it's an unspoken rule that you *don't* ask your parents. It's supposed to be a top secret place."

Sarah looked at me. "Did you tell your parents about it?"

"No," I said. I didn't add that a big part of me did want to tell them about the Barn as it was obviously a place that had heavily featured in Abby's life. Even if they weren't talking about her much I suspected they were searching for answers just as much as I was.

"Where did they think you were then?" she asked.

I looked down at my hands. "I told them I was at yours." I shot her an apologetic smile. "Sorry."

She didn't say anything but I knew from the way her face paled that she was upset. I chewed on the inside of my cheek. I felt a pang of guilt for not inviting her to go with me.

"I didn't think you'd want to go," I said.

Sarah didn't look at me.

Callum arrived with our mochas and Jill thanked him with too much enthusiasm.

"Do you know if he's single?" Jill asked me when he was back behind the counter.

"No," I said, glancing over at him. "I think he might be. He's never mentioned a girlfriend anyway."

"Hmm," Jill looked thoughtful. "D'you reckon he'd want to come with us to the Barn?"

"Probably not," I said. "He didn't really like it."

Jill frowned. "Damn. That would have been a good way to ask him out without asking him out, you know?"

I shot Sarah a knowing smirk. Jill was never shy in asking anyone out. Sarah's lips twitched slightly but she refused to commit to a full smile.

I spooned off some marshmallows from my mocha and took a sip. The caffeine and chocolate soothed my body instantly.

The bell chimed on the door and a strange sensation washed over me, the hairs on the back of my neck tingling. I took another sip.

Jill nudged me, mocha slopping over the edge of my mug.

"Watch it." I mopped at my chin with a napkin.

"Isn't that the singer from that band?"

I turned my head just as Rob walked over to the counter. Callum's face darkened and he folded his arms. My heart did a little flip. I gulped more of my mocha, feeling my face flush.

"Uh, I think so," I said. I put my cup back down, aware that my hands were beginning to shake.

Sarah looked at him, then at me. "Who is he?"

"He's an art student. He created the Barn and he plays in a band," Jill answered for me. "Now *he* is a total hottie. Like film star gorgeous."

Sarah was still looking at me. My face was burning. I wanted to run through to the back, away from her scrutinising gaze and definitely before Rob noticed me.

I risked another glance at the counter, at the exact moment

Rob turned his head to look directly at me. He put his hands in his pockets and his eyebrows twitched a gesture, like hello, or of recognition at least.

Oh god. I looked away, back at my mocha. The cream was dissolving into marbled swirls. I focused on the patterns, trying to distract myself from his presence.

I heard Callum opening and closing the till and Rob saying thanks. He strode over to the table beside us and chose to sit at the seat which faced me. He looked at me and I tried to ignore him.

"He's kind of staring at you," Jill said out the corner of her mouth, her lips stretching like a comedy cartoon character.

It would have been funny if it wasn't *him* and if I didn't feel so... affected...by him. What was that feeling? Was it attraction? It felt like a panic attack.

Sarah couldn't resist and turned to look at him.

I sank a little lower in my chair.

"Hello!" Rob waved at Sarah and her head snapped back round, eyes wide.

"I think he saw you looking," Jill whispered.

Sarah shot her a look. "Why is he staring at you, Kat?"

"No idea," I said. I tried to position myself so that Sarah's head was blocking my view of him. He shifted in his seat so that his face came back into view. A smirk played on his lips and annoyance sparked inside of me.

I stood up abruptly and Jill and Sarah looked at me in surprise.

"I should get back to work," I said, looking over at Callum who was standing with his arms still folded, watching Rob. "I'll speak to you both soon." I picked up my cup and headed across the cafe, straight through to the kitchen. I placed my cup in the sink and then opened the fridge, sticking my head inside to cool down.

"You alright, dear?" Mrs Hodge asked, concern in her voice.

"Fine," I called from inside the fridge. I moved some items around, pretending to be looking for something.

"Kat," Callum shouted from out front some minutes later.

I breathed in some more cold air.

"Callum's calling you, dear," Mrs Hodge said.

I reluctantly shut the fridge door and Callum appeared, looking irritated.

"Someone wants to talk to you."

"Oh." I walked out from the kitchen, expecting to see Jill and Sarah. Instead I nearly walked straight into Rob, who was hovering at the edge of the counter.

"Hi," he said.

I swallowed. "Hi." I looked to see if Jill and Sarah were still at their table but all that remained were their empty cups.

"You left last night without saying goodbye," Rob said.

I could feel Callum's gaze burning into my back.

I walked out into the cafe, steering Rob away from the counter.

"It was getting late. I had to go home," I said.

He looked over my shoulder. "What's with cafe boy there?"

"Who...Callum?" I blinked.

"He's not very friendly. Is he your boyfriend?"

"No." I frowned.

Rob scratched his chin. "What time d'you finish in here?"

"Four." My heartbeat quickened.

"Okay. I'll see you then." He hesitated like he was going to say something else then he turned and walked away.

I watched him walk up the stairs and out the door. *He'd see me then?* I felt a mixture of excitement and irritation, that he presumed I would be free to see him... And why was he coming back...was he coming back to take me out somewhere?

"That guy is weird," Callum muttered as he slipped past me to fetch empty cups. "Watch him, Kat."

I doubted I had a choice. He appeared to be already watching me.

CHAPTER 6

Four o'clock approached and I took my time clearing tables, throwing sidelong glances towards the door. Four fifteen appeared and he still hadn't.

"Don't you want to go home today?" Callum took a cup from my hand.

"Hmm?" I looked up at him, my attention still half on the door.

"Everything okay?" he asked.

His face came into full focus. I detected real concern in his eyes and it took me by surprise. He had kind eyes; bright, like there were no complications hidden behind them. "Yeah, I'm fine. Really."

"You up to anything tomorrow evening?" he asked.

I tried to remember what shifts I'd been given this week. "I think I'm free."

"D'you fancy coming along to a poetry night at my University Union? It starts about seven thirty. I thought it might let you see the more sophisticated side of university life."

"Okay, sure," I nodded, a little taken aback by the invitation. I wasn't even sure non university students were allowed into their unions. "Should I just see you there?"

"You'll need me to sign you in. I can swing by your house and pick you up if you want?"

"Okay," I said.

"Cool. I'll pick you up about seven?"

"Okay," I nodded. I glanced at the door again then looked back at the clock. Four twenty. He obviously wasn't going to show. I walked through to get my stuff and headed outside. My heart did a little flip when I spotted him standing further up the street, looking in the window of the local wool shop. I took a deep breath and walked up to him.

"Thinking of knitting a scarf?" I said.

He turned around slowly. "Maybe." He looked back at the shop front. "The shops round here are very twee."

"It's a twee town," I said, suddenly feeling self-conscious.

"I thought you finished at four," he said.

"I got held up," I lied, not wanting to admit for one minute I had expected him to come in for me.

"Want to go a walk?" he asked.

"Okay," I shrugged.

"Cool." He started to walk and I fell in step beside him, trying not to stare. He looked even more striking in daylight. A million miles from the boys I was used to socialising with at school. My palms started to sweat.

"D'you smoke?" he asked.

"No," I said, taken aback by his question.

"Me neither," he said. There was a silence and I looked at him, wondering why he had asked.

"Your sister smoked."

I frowned. "No she didn't."

He slid his hands into his jacket pockets. "She smoked when she hung about with some of us at the Barn. I think it was Michael's influence. She never actually had a packet of her own cigarettes when I think about it. She just borrowed some from him...if that makes you feel any better."

"What makes you think it would make me feel bad?"

He shrugged. "Just a guess...that as a non smoker you wouldn't really like the idea of your twin lighting up."

An image of Abby with a cigarette in her mouth flashed in my mind and he was right; I didn't like it.

"Did she take drugs?" I asked quietly.

He kicked a stone in front of him. "Maybe. I never gave her anything but there's stuff around the place. I think there were times she acted a bit over-affectionate."

"What do you mean?" I frowned.

"You know, like everything is beautiful, your hair is sooo beautiful. Like she'd taken some E." He looked at me and I felt like he was waiting for some reaction. I didn't say anything, trying to keep my face expressionless. I *didn't* know. I knew zero about drugs. I shivered, not liking the taints appearing around my memories of Abby.

He stopped walking and looked down at me. "You okay? Am I upsetting you?"

I looked into his eyes and momentarily forgot the question. "I'm fine. It's just, weird hearing things…I didn't know…"

"Have you been to visit her grave?" he asked.

I was thrown by his question. "No...I...didn't want to go." I didn't add that my parents went every weekend and that I preferred to talk to her in my head. There was something too final about looking at a concrete stone confirming her end date.

"Want to go with me just now?"

I hesitated, an image of gravestones flashing in front of my eyes.

"It's okay if you don't. I just thought it might make it easier... having someone go with you," he said softly.

"Do you go sometimes?" I asked.

He nodded. "I like to sit at sunset sometimes, singing her songs she used to like."

I snorted. "Are you being serious?"

"Why wouldn't I be?"

"It just sounds a bit…cheesy…" I said.

"I sing her Slipknot." He adopted a mock serious expression.

I smiled wryly. "Her favourite."

He folded his arms. "So, what do you say, Kat? You want to come with me?"

"Okay," I nodded and I felt something lift inside of me, knowing he wanted to go with me, knowing that someone else was sitting thinking about her sometimes.

"So how come you weren't in school that day I saw you in the cafe?" he asked.

"I don't need to be there. I got good exam results from last year."

"Abby always said you were the smart sister."

"She talked about me?" I said.

"You sound surprised."

"It's just when you first saw me...I thought you looked so shocked... like you didn't even realise that Abby had a twin."

"I knew. She talked about you a lot. I guess I wasn't prepared for how identical you are, even although you're not..." He scratched his head. "I'm not really articulating that very well. I guess what I mean is it was just disconcerting...like Abby was suddenly resurrected as some darker image of herself."

Darker? I knew what he meant but it made me sound like some demon version of my sister. "You acted like you didn't really know her that well when we first spoke. But it sounds like you were pretty close."

He shrugged. "I'm fascinated by a lot of people who hang out at the Barn. We seem to attract complicated and interesting characters."

I frowned. I had the feeling he was being intentionally evasive about her. "Did you go out with her?"

Silence. His face was a blank mask of non emotion. It fascinated me, how hard he was to read.

"I don't have relationships with people," he said.

I laughed. "What do you mean; you *don't have relationships with people*?"

"Just that. I don't like to get too involved with anyone."

I looked at him curiously. "Why not?"

He let out a long breath. "You ask a lot of questions."

"I too am fascinated by people."

"Touché."

I ran a hand along the railings as we approached the cemetery. "My guess is that you sleep with people and then you move on, breaking some hearts along the way."

He raised an eyebrow. "That would be a bit of cliché."

I wanted to ask him if he'd slept with Abby, if he had broken her heart, but I wasn't sure I really wanted to know.

"Come on, this is a quicker way in." He reached for my hand, pulling me towards a gap in the cemetery railings, and I recoiled in surprise. He turned to look at me, amusement in his eyes.

I flushed with embarrassment.

"I don't bite," he said.

I tried to arrange my face into what I hoped was a non-plussed expression. I stepped in front of him and squeezed through the gap. "Ladies first," I said, my voice portraying none of the somersaults turning in my stomach.

A breeze swept through the trees and blew my hair around my face as I stood looking at the rows of gravestones. A shiver ran up my legs and I folded my arms around my body, trying not to think of Abby lying underground. It wasn't her. It was just a shell. I thought of Abby's essence as being everywhere, with me as I walked; in the trees, in the stars. Like she was always there, watching me. Was she watching me? I wondered if she would be jealous, if she could see me now with Rob.

"This way." Rob nodded in the direction of the big oak tree at the bottom of a winding path.

I walked slowly, glancing at the headstones as I passed. I stopped at a marbled stone. It looked new. I read the inscription: Martin Anderson, beloved son and brother, your memory lives on in our hearts. 1995-2014. *He was one of them.* I stuffed my hands in my pockets, a shudder running through my body. A conversation I'd had with Abby flashed into my head.

"Don't you think there's something romantic about being buried in a large graveyard?"

I looked up from my book and watched Abby throw herself down on my bedroom floor, kicking her shoes off.

"What are you talking about?" I was trying to memorise dates of wars and the numbers kept jumping around in my head, forming wrong sequences.

"There's something amazing about walking around the graves at sunset, it's so quiet and atmospheric. Like you can totally see the bigger picture of life and death. I love reading the inscriptions and seeing names etched into a stone, like they can live forever. I want to be buried when I die."

I shot her a look. "When did you become so poetic?"

"Recent conversations with people have made me see things in a different way." She jumped up and twirled around my room, her hair a flash of gold. "Kat, are you listening?" She tugged at my hand, trying to get me to engage with her enthusiasm. "You can't ever let my body be burned, okay? I want to be remembered."

"Hey."

I blinked and looked up at Rob. Tears distorted my vision and I rubbed at my eyes, hoping he hadn't noticed. I turned away, my breath coming out in gasps.

"Look," he laid a hand on my shoulder. "I didn't want to upset you bringing you here. We can leave..."

I shook my head. She had got her request. A subconscious part of my brain had remembered to communicate her wish when the funeral arrangements blurred past. I just hadn't remembered the whole conversation until now. Her words made me realise she must have already been thinking about her death at that point. A month... weeks before? Why? *There is nothing romantic about this, Abby,* I wanted to scream at her. She had seemed so happy that day, her usual hyper self.

"That gravestone over there...he was one of the suicides," I said.

Rob glanced at Martin Anderson's grave. "I guess they'll all be here."

Would they all be here? I thought back to funerals, tried to think if the crematorium had been mentioned. I realised that a lot of people had talked about visiting graves to lay flowers.

"It's kind of strange, if they all got buried," I frowned. "It's more common now to get cremated...don't you think?"

Rob shrugged. "No idea."

"Did Martin go to the Barn?" I asked.

Rob looked down at his name. "Hmm...not sure I recall someone called Martin."

I studied his face. There was something about the tone of his voice that made me wonder.

"Come on, Abby's grave is this way." Rob started to head further down the path. I watched his back as he walked, creases forming in his leather jacket. His black jeans were frayed at the bottom, Converses scuffed around the heels. *Abby fell in love with you.* The feeling hit me with certainty, almost like she had momentarily reached inside of me, sprinkling her emotions into my gut.

"I've changed my mind," I said.

He turned his head in surprise. He waited for me to say something.

I folded my arms. "It doesn't feel right. I...I'm not ready."

He turned round and walked back towards me. "Okay."

I waited to see if he was going to probe me further; he didn't. "Let's go somewhere else."

"I know the perfect place," he smiled and I felt a part of me falling inside that smile as I followed him.

CHAPTER 7

Images I didn't want to remember flashed through my head like electric shocks when I realised Rob was leading me in the direction of Eddison Woods.

"Are we going to the Barn?"

"Ten out of ten, Sherlock," Rob said. He turned round, realising I'd stopped walking. "What's up?" He looked at me, then at the woods.

"Can we go round the long way?" I said.

"Sure."

I was relieved he understood without asking for an explanation.

We walked on in silence and I started to relax in his company. Being with someone with minimal words calmed me.

"It must have been rough being the one to find her," Rob said.

The calm instantly melted away. Everything tilted in front of me, the images returning, swirling around my head like a recurring nightmare on a loop.

Running through the woods, my legs on fire from running so far and so fast but only being half aware of the physical pain...the mental anguish taking over...the breathless panic and the out-of-body sensation of knowing something, knowing where to find her. Like part of her was clinging on, whispering to me and projecting images into my head so I would know where she was. Twins' telepathy. We used to share that bond, fleetingly, as twelve-year-olds when we were experimental with things like that, when we liked having an intimate bond. We tried the shapes test. Drawing a triangle and loving the thrill of turning over her paper and finding it matched.

There was no thrill in my certainty that night. Finding her in the woods, hanging from a tree. She had on muddy pink All Stars; her shoelace was undone and I had an irrational compulsion to climb up the tree and reach over and tie it for her…

"I read in the paper that you nearly found her in time."

I jolted back to the here and now, Rob coming into focus. Anger sparked inside me. "Why would you even bring that up?"

His face paled. I wondered how that was even possible when his skin was already alabaster.

I stormed on ahead.

He took his time catching me up. "I was just…thinking. It must have been hard."

"Biggest understatement ever," I said through clenched teeth.

"You're right. I'm sorry."

"They told us later, after the post-mortem, that she must have only been dead about ten minutes before I arrived." I shook my head. "Ten minutes. How can they even tell these things? And how do journalists get to know these details to print in the paper? I didn't want to know. I didn't want to find her."

I realised I was shouting and Rob was trying to place his hands on my arms. I lashed out at him, hitting his hands away. "She was so selfish doing it. I hate her for leaving us like this." I could hear wailing sounds like a distant animal, disorientated when I realised they were coming from me.

"It's okay." Rob pulled me towards him and I tried to resist but he was strong. His arms circled my shoulders and I gave in, allowing myself to lean into him. He stood holding me and I could smell that same muskiness from the night at the Barn, feel his warmth. I pulled back, realising that his t-shirt was soaked. I wiped at my eyes. He pulled a paper napkin from his jacket pocket and I took it, blowing my nose loudly. He raised an eyebrow and smirked. I managed a smile.

"Feel better?" he asked. I tried to hand him back his napkin but he recoiled in mock horror. "Disgusting."

I smiled, scrunching it up and stuffing it in my bag. "I can imagine my make-up has seen better days." I rummaged around in my bag and pulled out a compact. Rubbing at the black smudges under my eyes wiped the remainder of my eye liner away. I snapped the mirror shut.

Rob looked at me, a strange expression on his face…of recognition, of remembering someone else.

"I do feel angry with her you know," I said, my body relaxing with the confession. "Everyone expects me to be sad all the time. Of course I'm devastated…but there's so much anger…"

"It's healthy to feel anger. You shouldn't feel bad about it," he said.

"It was horrific finding her there in the woods. And she knew someone was going to have to find her like that…I know she'd never have thought it would be me. But anyone, having to see that…" I didn't go on to tell Rob that I'd had nightmares for weeks afterwards. Or even worse, dreams where the ending changed; I found her in time and saved her. Waking from those had been more upsetting as I'd had to face the reality over and over that I hadn't saved her. That I had been too late.

Rob touched my arm. "I doubt she'd have thought about how horrible that would be."

"The way the papers ran with the story that I nearly found her in time.… It made me feel guilty that I didn't find her sooner. That I didn't even know why…"

"You shouldn't feel guilty." His fingers brushed against mine. "It wasn't your fault."

"I can't help but think that she wanted me to find her. That she was calling out to me to find her, to help her. That's the hardest part, that I couldn't *help* her." I shook my head. "She was always the sensitive one; I should have been there for her, looked after her more…"

"Kat," Rob whispered my name. He brushed my hair back from

my face and I peered up at him. He gazed into my eyes and he looked lost for a moment, like he was drifting through memories. He quickly turned away and I realised I'd been holding my breath… that I'd been hoping he might kiss me. I stuffed my hands into my pockets so that there was no risk of contact again.

His face resumed a mask of non emotion as we picked up pace and walked the rest of the way to the Barn in silence.

In daylight the building looked more run down, the wood around the edges beginning to rot. The corrugated sheets of metal surrounding some of the walls and roof was rusting. Rob led me to the doorway at the side and knocked on it loudly.

"Don't you have a key?" I asked.

"Yup. But the door will be bolted from the inside if someone's in." He must have noticed my frown as he added, "We don't like getting unexpected visitors. Andy Warhol let anyone wander into his factory and he got shot by a radical feminist."

"I doubt we have to worry about guns around here," I scoffed.

"No, but there're still a lot of people who wouldn't be welcome."

A little thrill ran up my spine as I realised I must be welcome. "So you did model this place on the Factory then?"

Rob nodded. "You know much about Andy Warhol?"

I shook my head. "Just that he liked Campbell's soup."

Rob smiled.

There was the sound of metal sliding against wood as the door opened a crack.

"Magic word?" a gruff voice commanded.

"Fuck off, Michael."

"Those are definitely not the magic words."

Rob pushed at the door and Michael relented and opened it fully, looking me up and down. His lingering gaze unnerved me and I felt Rob tense beside me, as if he too did not appreciate Michael paying me attention.

"Well, hello Kitty Kat."

Rob shot him a look. He reached behind me to close and re-bolt the door.

We followed Michael up the stairs. As we reached the open space at the top it also looked different in daylight. Music was playing quietly from a turntable set up beside the sofas. A woman sat cross-legged on one of the sofas, plaiting her hair. Two guys sat on a white rug on the floor beside her, one of them tuning a guitar.

At the back of the room, easels were set up and two girls stood painting. One of them had on cut-off jeans and a bra. I blushed, wondering how she could just stand there, so unselfconscious. No one was paying any attention to her and I wondered if people here often stood around in their underwear.

The woman on the sofa looked over as we approached.

"Hey Rob," she called. Her smile had a hint of longing to it, and I felt a pang of jealousy.

Rob waved and continued walking. Michael sat down on the sofa beside the woman and picked up a bottle of beer on the table beside them. Rob turned his head to check that I was following and led me behind white sheets to one side of the easels. Paints, brushes and canvasses were set out on tables with a sink in the middle. Rob took off his jacket and started to wash brushes in the sink.

Paintings and drawings were pinned up along the walls and I circled the space, looking at them in more detail. I stopped at a small pen drawing of a girl's face and traced a finger around the eyes and the lips. "Abby."

Rob turned his head sharply. "Sorry, I forgot that was there." He reached over my shoulder and took the picture off the wall.

"It's fine, you don't need to take it down." Sadness flashed across his face as he looked at the picture.

"Did you draw it?"

"Yeah," he said. "You want it?"

I shook my head. "You should keep it."

He held it out to me. "I don't want it."

I took the picture and slipped it into my bag. Another image of a girl caught my eye and I turned to get a closer look.

"Hey," Rob touched my arm and held up clenched fists to my face. "Pick one."

I shot him a bemused look then gestured to his left hand. "That one."

He unclenched the fist to reveal a tube of paint. "Magenta. Good choice." He unclenched his other hand. "Much better than Canary yellow."

"What's it for?"

"The background colour for my new piece," he said.

I glanced down at the tattoo running up his arm, realising the text was Latin. "What does your tattoo say?"

He touched the tattoo, as if he'd forgotten about its existence. *"Aut viam inveniam aut faciam."*

I shot him a withering smile. "I meant what does it say in English?"

"I'll either find a way or make one."

He grabbed my arm and pulled me over to the rows of paints. "You choose some for yourself too. I'll get you set up outside."

I shook my head. "I don't know how to paint."

"It's not about knowing," he said. He looked me straight in the eye, his gaze penetrating. "It's about feeling."

He picked up an easel and a blank canvas and waited for me to choose some paints, then we walked back out into the open space and he set me up beside the girl with the bra. She glanced at me then went back to painting. I was glad she wasn't expecting me to make conversation with her.

Rob brought out some brushes for me and a tub of water. He laid them at my feet. He glanced up and smiled. "Don't look so worried, Kat."

"Easy for you to say," I hissed. "You're all fecking art students."

He straightened up and unscrewed the top of one of my paints. "You don't need to paint anything great. Just go with what feels good. Have fun...let yourself go."

I took the tube of paint from him and squirted a blob of bright blue onto my canvas. "Brush?"

He handed me a long flat brush and I attacked the blob of paint, smudging it roughly across the canvas.

"Amazing." He observed the mess with mock admiration. "Keep it up."

He disappeared back behind the screen and I glanced at the girl's canvas. She was painting something abstract with lots of colour. It looked weird but professional. I looked back at my canvas. Primary school.

Rob set up his easel beside mine but angled it so I couldn't see his canvas.

"Why are you blocking my view?" I asked.

"I don't like anyone seeing my work 'til it's done," he said.

"Don't you have studios at the art school in the city?" I asked, opening a new tube of paint...teal. I squirted a smaller amount onto the canvas and began to dab at it tentatively.

"Yeah. All my coursework is over there."

"Are you studying painting?"

"No."

I waited for him to elaborate. "Do I have to keep asking until I get it right?"

He flashed me one of his half smiles. "I'm studying sculpture. I like to paint when I'm here though."

"Do you live in the city?"

He nodded. "I share a flat with Michael."

"How did you find this place?"

"I was doing a project studying trees so came to Eddison Woods and chanced upon here. Thought it looked like a decent place and it was up for let so we took it."

I wanted to ask more about how they converted the place but had the feeling Rob wouldn't want to tell me much, not in front of the others anyway.

"What year are you in?" I asked.

He looked up from his easel. "How about you write a list of questions and I'll write an autobiography for you?"

"Sorry, I'm just curious." I shrugged.

"I've just started second year."

I thought for a moment. "How old does that make you then?"

"Eighteen and eight months. Did you think I was older?"

"No," I lied. The fact he added in the eight months made me think he wanted to appear older.

I moved closer beside him. He turned his easel even further round the other way. I gave him a withering look. "I'm not trying to look at your picture. I just wondered who those girls are..." I gestured towards bra girl. "And why she's standing in her bra."

He smirked. "That's Leah and Josie. They're painting students. Josie values freedom of expression." He shrugged. "We encourage it in here. Does it make you uncomfortable?"

I considered lying. "A bit."

"Poor repressed Kat."

I frowned. "Don't mock me." I moved back to my canvas, dabbing at the paint with more force.

Loud bangs echoed across the room and everyone paused, disorientated. I stared at Rob. More bangs; this time it was obvious it was fists pounding against a door.

"Alright, alright," Michael shouted, getting up off the sofa. He looked over in our direction and Rob walked across the room, both of them heading down the stairs to see who was at the door.

I laid down my paints and brush and walked towards the stairs, hearing animated female voices and someone sobbing.

"It's alright. Calm down." Rob's voice was reassuring.

"He's okay."

Footsteps clambered on the stairs and Chloe and Lisa appeared. I stepped forward, straining to see who was with them.

Rob and Michael came back into view, holding a boy between them. His hair hung over his face but did little to obscure the bruising purpling across his cheeks, and the blood running from his nose. My first thought was suicide but then my brain kicked in and realised his injuries were obviously inflicted from an attack.

"We found him by the loch…" Lisa was babbling. "He said it was some boys in hoodies."

Rob lowered him onto one of the sofas and tipped his head back. He turned to Chloe. "Go and get some tissues and a bowl of water."

She nodded, her face ashen. She glanced at me on her way past and not in a friendly way.

"Who is it? Is he okay?" I grabbed her arm.

She shrugged off my grip. "It's Tom."

Tom? I looked back at the boy, recognition dawning. I pulled out my mobile from my bag, hands shaking, and dialled Callum's number.

CHAPTER 8

"Where is he?"

I straightened up, opening the door to the Barn as Callum rushed out of the woods towards me. "He's upstairs."

Callum brushed past me, taking the stairs two at a time. I hurried after him. "He's okay, Callum. Just a bit shaken up."

Callum turned his head. "Who did it?"

"Lisa and Chloe said it was some boys down by the loch." I ran up the last few steps, trying to catch up with Callum as he strode across the room towards Michael.

"Who're you?" Michael frowned. The woman from earlier touched Michael's arm, as if to calm him.

"This is Callum, Tom's brother," I said.

"Where is he?" Callum repeated.

Michael stubbed out a cigarette onto a coaster. "He's in a back room with Rob. I'll go and get him."

Callum started to follow him and Michael turned round. "I said I'd get him."

"And I'll come with you," Callum said.

Michael hesitated, then kept walking.

I headed over to the sofa and took a seat beside Lisa, who was chewing her nails. I watched as the woman walked over to a coat stand, slipped on a leather jacket then hurried downstairs, clearly wanting to avoid any drama.

Chloe sat on the floor by Lisa's feet, lighting a cigarette. She shifted slightly when I sat down and stared straight ahead.

"Did you see the boys who did it?" I asked Lisa.

She shook her head. "We just saw Tom, lying on the ground. At first we thought..." Her words trailed off and I didn't need her to finish the sentence to know what they must have thought.

"D'you reckon they could have been from Eddison High?" I asked.

"Probably," Chloe said, blowing spirals of smoke up into the air. "There's a bunch of neds in Tom's year who try to start fights all the time. I saw a couple of them shoving Tom against his locker last week."

I felt a pang of sympathy for him. "Does he have friends in school?"

Chloe shrugged. "I guess so. I see him wandering the corridors with those grunge geeks, Brian and Ian..."

A door opened across the room and I heard Callum raising his voice.

"Calm down..." Rob followed him out of the room.

"How d'you think giving him whisky is going to make him feel better? He needs antiseptic cream to put on those cuts, not to get drunk with you." Callum stood eye to eye with Rob and I realised he must be the same height as him...I'd imagined Rob to be taller.

"Whisky is good for shock," Rob said. "And I thought it might numb the pain a bit. I'm not trying to get him drunk."

"He was drinking out the bottle," Callum said.

"Shut up, Callum." Tom appeared, looking a little less fragile. "He was just trying to help."

Chloe dashed over to them. "You alright?"

Tom nodded, blushing slightly. "Thanks for your help."

"No problem, kiddo," Chloe said. She smiled at Rob and I wondered if she'd said 'kiddo' for his benefit, to make herself appear older.

"You know you could get done for giving underage kids alcohol," Callum said.

Rob's face darkened.

"I'm not a kid..." Tom protested.

"You're sixteen," Callum growled.

"I think you should leave now," Rob said.

"Gladly." Callum nudged Tom. "Let's get you home."

I stood up as they passed. Rob shot me a questioning stare with traces of anger when he realised I was going to leave. I wanted to tell him I was just concerned that Tom was okay, but not when Chloe was standing beside him, scrutinising my every move. I gave him a little wave and then I hurried down the stairs after Callum.

"You don't need to come with us," Callum said.

"I just wanted to make sure…everything was okay," I said.

Once outside, Tom stormed ahead. "I'm going the long way home," He shouted to Callum.

"Fine, I'll go that way too," Callum shouted back.

"You seemed pretty angry in there," I said.

"That guy, Rob, just annoys me. He's so fecking arrogant."

"He's not really. He's just quite…self-assured."

Callum rolled his eyes. "I don't like the fact he's in there boozing with sixteen-year-olds. It's creepy and predatory."

I laughed. "Jesus, you make him sound like a paedo or something. He's not that much older than me."

Callum stopped abruptly and I nearly tripped over him. "I told you there was no need to come with us. Why don't you go back inside with James Dean?"

"Fine. I'll leave you to it." I walked on ahead in the direction of home. Tom turned to look at me in surprise as I stomped past him.

"Kat."

I ignored the call.

"Kat, wait up," Callum shouted, running to catch up with me. He caught my arm, forcing me to turn to look at him. "I'm sorry. I didn't mean to snap at you."

I sighed. "I was just concerned." I lowered my voice so Tom couldn't hear. "Chloe said she saw some boys in Tom's year shoving him against a locker the other week."

Callum frowned, turning to glance at his brother. "D'you reckon he's getting bullied?"

"Maybe," I said. "You could try talking to him about it."

"Stop talking about me." Tom glared at us both as he overtook us again.

Callum sighed. "I can see it's going to be easy having a heart to heart."

"Persevere. It'll be worth it," I said, wanting to tell him that I wished I'd had more heart to hearts with Abby, then maybe I could have helped her. "Why was he walking around the woods anyway? I thought he'd still be grounded."

Callum shrugged. "Probably sneaked out."

"Was Mrs Hodge okay about you leaving early?" I looked at my watch. "I could go back and help her close up."

Callum shook his head. "She was fine about it. What were you doing at the Barn anyway? D'you go there a lot?"

I could tell he was trying to sound casual, but clearly wasn't happy about the prospect of me spending time there either. "First time I've been back," I said. "It seems different during the day. Art students use the space to paint."

"In their underwear." Callum made a face.

I smiled. "Yeah. That's a bit weird."

"Do you paint?" he asked.

I laughed. "No, although I was attempting to."

"I guess it's good to have that creative space. I wonder how they could afford to buy the place and maintain it."

"I don't know...I think they pay rent... They do charge an entry fee I guess on the weekends," I said, remembering the girl with the tin.

"I doubt students are going to contribute much," Callum scoffed.

We reached a turning in the road and stopped as we each had to take an opposite direction to get home.

"So I'll pick you up tomorrow at seven?" Callum said.

"Sure." I nodded. "You remember where my house is?"

"I remember."

"I hope Tom's okay."

Callum looked over my shoulder and I turned to follow his gaze, watching Tom as he walked on down the road, hands in pockets, head down. "He'll be okay."

"See you."

When I arrived home I could hear the radio on in the kitchen and smells of dinner floated out from under the door. Proper dinner... like lasagne. I couldn't remember the last time Mum had cooked. I pushed the door open wider, watching as she fluffed salad in a bowl.

"Hi," I said.

Mum turned around and her mouth opened in surprise when she saw me. The bowl slid from her hands and I rushed forward.

"Mum..." I bent down to pick up slithers of lettuce.

"Sorry." She crouched down beside me. She stared into my eyes intently, like she was looking for something. "You startled me."

I straightened up, remembering that my tears had washed off my eyeliner and I was probably looking too much like Abby. "Sorry." I sat down at the table. "Dinner smells nice."

"I thought it had been a while since we had a proper dinner together," she said. "You can set the table if you like."

Relief washed over me. We hadn't sat down together at the table for dinner since Abby's death. Maybe Mum was finally starting to feel better. I started to clear the fruit bowl and magazines off the table.

"You're back late from work. Did they ask you to stay on?" Mum asked.

"No. I just met up with...some friends," I said, pulling out cutlery from the drawer. I started to take out four forks then let one drop, swallowing the lump threatening to form in my throat.

"How is Sarah? I've not seen her around much lately."

"Oh, she's fine," I said, not bothering to correct her presumption.

"You should invite her over sometime," she suggested.

I didn't say anything, thinking I would rather wait to see if this show of normality was likely to continue first. Sarah was uncomfortable enough around me, never mind having to walk into a house which was suffocating from mourning.

The front door slammed shut and I heard keys being dropped in the bowl on the shelf in the hall. Dad walked into the kitchen and smiled. "Something smells nice." He walked up behind Mum and nuzzled her neck. "Not only the dinner."

He laid down a cake box. "Dessert as requested."

Warmth spread across my shoulders, like an embrace, reassuring me things were going to be okay.

He turned his attention to me. "How's work going?" He helped me finish laying out the cutlery and sat down across the table from me.

"Okay." I nodded. "I've only managed to mess up people's orders a couple of times and I've passed my trial period. Mrs Hodge won't let me take a turn preparing the food yet but I'm sure I'll prove to her soon enough that I've got culinary skills."

Mum snorted. "How about proving it here first? Feel free to practice anytime."

"Maybe I will," I said, feeling bad for not thinking to take over the cooking lately. I hadn't really felt hungry enough to even care what was being served up to me.

Mum shot me a reassuring smile. "I don't mind teaching you a few things."

"That would be good," I said.

"Should be about done now."

Dad got up to help Mum take the lasagne out the oven and I watched them move together. They seemed closer than I'd seen them in ages. Mum didn't flinch at his touch; they were making eye contact, managing a smile.

"What happened to the salad?" Dad asked, noticing the half empty bowl.

"Oh, I dropped it. There's some left in the bag in the fridge," Mum said.

They joined me at the table and we avoided eye contact. I tried not to look at the vacant chair.

"Hmm, delicious." Dad chewed on a piece of lasagne.

I shovelled some into my mouth and for the first time in forever felt my tummy growl, not in protest, but from actual hunger. "This is great, Mum."

"I'm glad," she smiled, cutting up her own but not actually eating any.

We sat not talking, the sound of the radio filling the silence. I tried to think of things to say but all I could think of was the Barn, Rob...his paintings...the painting I'd found of Abby in her room. I wanted to ask them if they'd ever noticed it before but I was scared to mention her name in case it ruined their mood.

"Missing school?" Dad asked.

"No." I shook my head.

"Oh, that reminds me. Miss Rowan your guidance teacher called and left a message on Friday. She was just checking everything was okay and asked if you could go in sometime to sign your leavers form," Mum said.

"I didn't realise I had to sign one of those. I wonder if I can just get her to do it."

"It would be nice to go in and say goodbye to your teachers," Mum said.

I shrugged. It would be okay to see Miss Rowan but I doubted any of the others would really care that much. Most of them appreciated my studious grades but not my desire to spark off debates in their classes.

The phone rang and Mum started to get up. Dad laid his hand on hers. "Just leave it, Karen."

"It might be important," Mum said. He relented, loosening his grip.

She walked over to the phone hanging on the wall by the fridge and I listened as she answered.

There was a long pause after hello. I glanced at Dad but he was busy eating his dinner. Mum's grip tightened, her knuckles turning white.

"She's not here," she said, her voice breaking. She slammed the phone down.

Dad's chair scraped against the floor as he got up and walked over to her. Her shoulders slumped as she clung onto the kitchen counter.

"Who was it?" Dad asked.

Mum shook her head. "Some guy."

"What guy?" Dad's voice had a trace of anger in it.

"I don't know. I didn't ask him," Mum shot back at him.

The piece of food I had in my mouth suddenly felt heavy and tasteless. I spat it out onto my napkin. "Was he looking for Abby?" I asked quietly.

Dad shot me a look which translated as a sarcastic 'what do you think?'

"Excuse me." Mum brushed past Dad and walked out of the kitchen, closing the door behind her.

Dad scratched his head and walked back to the table, lowering himself slowly into his chair. He picked up his fork then laid it back down again.

I walked over to the phone and keyed in 1471.

"What are you doing?" Dad asked.

"I want to know who it was," I said, hearing *'You were called today at seven p.m...the caller withheld their number.'* I slammed the phone back down. "Who would call her? Everyone knows for God's sake. Who would do that?"

Dad sighed loudly. "I don't know, Kat," he said wearily. "Sit down and finish your dinner."

"I'm not hungry any more." I looked at the closed kitchen door, cursing whoever had phoned. Idiot.

"You want some cake?" Dad said, getting up and scraping the leftover food into the bin.

"No." I shook my head. "Maybe later?"

Dad nodded.

I left him to it, hurrying up the stairs to Abby's room. Distant sobs were floating down the hallway from Mum and Dad's room. *Don't cry, Mum.* I pleaded with her. I rested my head on Abby's door, closing my eyes. *Can you see what you've done to us?* I clenched my fist. *I really hope somewhere you can see what you've done to us.*

Cold air hit me when I stepped inside. I switched the light on and walked over to check the window; it was tightly shut. I pulled the curtains together and turned to survey the room.

As I sat down at her dressing table I glanced in the mirror, moving my face close to the glass and staring into my eyes.

"Somewhere, deep down inside, I know you're still here. I know you're still a part of me," I whispered. Staring intently, my reflection started to blur and I imagined seeing Abby in my place. I raised a hand and waved. The hand waved back a hello.

Why did you leave me?

The reflection stared back silently, offering no answers.

I turned away from the mirror and flopped down on Abby's bed, sinking down into the duvet. I buried my face in the bedclothes and inhaled traces of her perfume, like she was embracing me from some far off place. My heart twisted. *I miss you so much. Didn't you think about how much I would miss you?* I grabbed a pillow and threw it across the room. A piece of paper fluttered to the ground, falling under her bed. I reached underneath and pulled it out, smoothing the crinkles. The writing on it stood out immediately as Abby's; distinctive loops across the page.

A date was written in the top corner: *February 4th...*

An extract of her journal. My heart soared. I ripped off all of the pillows, searching underneath for more. I tore the sheets off the bed, searched underneath the mattress, underneath the bed. Nothing. Just this one page...but it was something.

I glanced back at the mirror. *Thank you.* I smiled and the girl in the mirror smiled back.

CHAPTER 9

The words seeped into my dreams and faded images played out scenes of distorted memories. Abby and me sitting cross-legged, laughing as we watched a film in my room...then standing in a shaded wood; Abby crying, me crying, holding out hands to one another and a dark swirl winding faster and faster between us, pulling her away from me.

No, I screamed. My eyes flew open and I sat up, gasping. My heart pounded against my chest and I wiped away the tears streaming down my cheeks.

The house was silent and light streamed in through the windows, signifying morning. I looked at my clock; eleven a.m. Usually, I woke up when Mum and Dad were getting ready for work but I hadn't fallen asleep until a few hours ago.

Abby's journal extract lay on my bedside table. The words were now firmly imprinted in my brain, after re-reading it again and again.

I love, love, love this place! :) It's like I can be me, Abby, not an inferior half of brilliance. The art students are so amazing – they seem like they're interested in what I've got to say and have so many cool stories. And ***he*** *was asking about me. Lisa told me. I can't believe out of all those girls, uni students and everything!! (and some are totally gorgeous!) that he would notice* ***me****. And his friend is always talking to me too. Makes the guys in school seem sooo lame. I hate school just now. All the teachers keep holding Kat up as some example for me to follow. It makes me feel like a loser; like they look at me as if I'm the dumb blonde twin. I wish I could just hang out at the Barn all day. I'm so glad I found this place...I feel like they 'get' me...*

An inferior half of brilliance. What was she talking about…the teachers holding me up as an example? They shouldn't have been comparing us at all. I pulled my knees up to my chin, a horrible feeling twisting inside. It sounded like I had made her feel unhappy, made her feel inferior…which was insane. I was the geek; she was the goddess…popular, funny…and she was so smart too.

I picked up the extract, took one last glance and shoved it in my drawer, wishing more than ever that I could talk to Abby, to ask her what she'd been thinking.

I stood outside the school, looking up at the windows of my old Spanish class. I could picture Mrs Jannett inside, making over-enthusiastic hand gestures to emphasise the correct pronunciations. The sounds of an out of tune trombone floated out the open windows of the music department and everything suddenly felt a bit surreal, like I was standing on the outside of a life I had left behind a lot longer than just a few weeks ago.

The main door to reception opened and I held my breath, bracing myself for a teacher I knew to bombard me with enquiring hellos. I was relieved to see it was a stranger, a visitor. She smiled and held the door for me. I hesitated then stepped inside.

Mrs Gibbs in the office was on the phone and none of the others were around so I stood waiting…and waiting. There were no lilts in the conversation and I had a feeling it would be a long one.

I headed on down the corridor in the direction of the English department. Miss Rowan might have a class and it might be people from my year – re-sits, like Sarah – who were in her class. I debated the situation in my head; peek in the window first before knocking…just to check.

The door to Miss Rowan's class lay open and I was relieved to find her sitting at her desk alone, with no class in sight.

I knocked quietly on the open door to get her attention.

It took her several seconds to look up and several more to realise it was me.

"Kat!" She stood up, a smile spreading across her face. "Come in. How are you?"

Her warmth calmed me and I smiled back. "I'm okay, thanks. How's everything here?"

"Good, everything is going well." She pulled a chair up beside her desk. "Sit down, tell me how you've been. Did your Mum tell you I called on Friday?"

I nodded. "She just remembered to tell me yesterday."

"It was good of you to come in."

"I wasn't going to," I confessed. Her mouth formed a curious 'Oh.' "It's just weird for me...coming back here..." I explained.

"Well, I'm really glad you did come in. I was surprised when you left suddenly. I was worried about you."

"I'm fine, really. I just decided I could do with some time out," I said. "I hadn't actually checked my certificate before you told me my results."

"Oh," she said. "I must have given you a nice surprise then."

"Yeah." I smiled. "It was just hard being here, you know, so I was glad I didn't have to stay."

She twirled her pen between her fingers. "How are things at home?"

I wasn't sure how to answer, not knowing how much I should share. "Difficult. It's like there's this sadness...everywhere. I know it'll take time, it just seems like things will never be normal again."

"Do you talk to your parents about Abby?"

I shook my head. "I'm scared to mention her name. They don't really want to talk about her."

"Give them time. I think it will help you all to talk about her, to remember the good things."

The journal flashed in my mind. I looked at Miss Rowan. "Did you ever compare us?"

She looked puzzled. "You and Abby? I'm not sure what you mean."

"Did you ever tell her to work harder, to get the grades I was getting?"

Miss Rowan laid down her pen. "No, Kat. I like to think I treated you both as individuals...do you feel I didn't?"

I shook my head. "No, you did. What about other teachers, d'you reckon they would have made her feel pressured?"

"I would hope not." She frowned. "Are you thinking she did feel pressure?"

I hesitated. I wasn't keen to let anyone know about the journal but I felt I could trust Miss Rowan. "I found an extract from her journal...she sounded like she felt inferior..." My voice broke and I dug my nails into the palms of my hand. Crying wasn't part of my plan for this visit.

Miss Rowan reached across and laid her hand comfortingly on my arm. "We all feel inferior from time to time, I'm sure; don't you?"

I nodded. "But Abby...she was so popular...and happy..."

"I'm sure Abby *was* happy most of the time. But no one is happy all the time...and a journal is the place you would use to vent all your emotions. D'you want to talk about anything else she'd written?"

I thought about telling Miss Rowan about the Barn but I knew telling an adult, especially a teacher, about everyone hanging around there would really open up the place to investigation. They would definitely ban under-agers from going, which would include me.

"No; it was only a short extract. There was nothing much in it really."

"Where did you find it?" she asked.

"Under her bed," I said, bending the truth slightly. Admitting I'd found it under her pillow would sound weird, like I had been sleeping in her bed.

"Weren't your parents looking for her journal? I remember them coming to the school; searching her locker. Did you show them the extract?"

"Not yet…I thought they might get too upset." That wasn't a complete lie, but it wasn't the main reason.

I glanced at the walls of her classroom, the posters comfortingly familiar. Last year when I'd been sitting here in this class seemed like a lifetime ago.

"I think Sarah misses you," Miss Rowan said carefully.

I miss her too, I wanted to say. Instead I kept a focus on her Romeo and Juliet poster.

"She'll be on a free period just now; probably be in the common room or library. You should stop by and say hello before you leave."

I nodded. "I got a job in Cake Tin," I said, changing the subject.

Miss Rowan smiled. "So I heard. I'll need to come in sometime and sample your coffee. I've heard it's the best in town."

"Well, we don't have much competition," I said, picturing an old greasy spoon at the other end of the park and another cafe run by a very old man who hadn't even bothered to invest in a proper coffee-making machine.

"I'm glad you found a job, it's not easy to get one these days."

"I think I just got lucky, right place, right time." I had a suspicion that Mrs Hodge felt so sorry for me that she would have offered me a job regardless of whether she needed extra help or not.

The bell rang and it didn't take long for a rush of people to burst out into the corridor. I stood up. "You got a class now?"

Miss Rowan nodded. "Fifth year."

"Do you have a Tom Riley in your class?"

"Tom, yes, the new boy. Why d'you ask?"

"I work with his brother. He got beaten up yesterday by some boys, reckon they probably go here. Keep an eye on him would you?"

"Of course. Thanks for mentioning." She frowned, no doubt names of potential attackers filling her head.

"It was nice to see you, Miss Rowan," I said.

"You too, Kat. Mind and keep in touch."

Some pupils strode in, looking at me curiously. One of the girls shot me a sympathetic smile. I hurried out into the corridor, panicking at the idea of having to make small talk with anyone.

As I headed back to the office I glanced in at the library, just as the door swung open and Sarah and Jill walked out. My heart sank.

"Kat!" Jill squealed. "What the hell are you doing here?"

Sarah shot me a smile.

"I'm in to sign my leavers form," I said, feeling awkward standing in my black jeans and t-shirt. Their school uniforms made me feel like an outcast. "Where you off to?"

"Maths." Jill made a face.

"Music," Sarah said.

"Cool." I nodded.

"What you up to this evening?" Sarah asked, surprising me.

"Callum invited me to some poetry reading at his university."

"Oh." Sarah looked a bit disappointed.

"Callum...the hot guy you work with?" Jill's eyes nearly popped out of her head. "Can we come?"

"Jill," Sarah said, giving her a look.

"What?" Jill shot her a look back.

"It might be a date," Sarah hissed. She looked expectantly at me.

"No, it's not a date," I laughed. "I guess it would be okay for you to come along...I'm not sure how many people he can sign in..."

"Great! Where should we meet you?" Jill asked.

"He's picking me up at mine at seven," I said.

"Cool, see you then." Jill clapped her hands excitedly. "Can't wait!"

Sarah shot me an apologetic smile.

"Okay, see you then." I watched as Jill pulled Sarah along the corridor, half skipping as they went on their way.

Callum didn't know what he had let himself in for.

CHAPTER 10

"He's here!" Jill nearly knocked the ornaments off my windowsill as she turned and ran over to the mirror on my dresser, smoothing down her dark hair. "Think I've overdone my make-up?" She smacked her red lips together.

"You always over-do your make-up," Sarah said wryly, pulling a brush through her blonde curls.

The doorbell rang and I grabbed my bag. "Come on." I hurried out the room and ran downstairs before Mum had the chance to answer the door.

Callum stood in the doorway, smiling. He had on a navy jacket and his eyes seemed very blue in the light. "Hi Kat."

"Hi."

His smile faltered as I opened the door wider and Jill and Sarah said their hellos.

"Hi…?" He looked at me questioningly.

I shot him an apologetic smile. "Hope you don't mind but they asked to come along."

"Oh, okay, no problem," he said in a way that suggested he did mind.

Jill practically jumped out the door, making sure she was beside him on the walk down the drive.

"Bye, Mum," I shouted, not waiting for any response before slamming the door shut.

"I think he was hoping to get you alone," Sarah whispered as we followed behind.

I dismissed her comment. "We're just friends."

"What about that Rob guy?"

My face flushed. "What about him?"

"He seemed overly fascinated with you in the cafe yesterday. He's extremely good looking, don't you think?"

"Hmm," I said, trying to keep my expression neutral.

"Did he know Abby?"

I nodded. "She apparently used to go to the Barn a lot."

Sarah didn't say anything, but I could tell her mind was ticking over, probably wondering the same thing as me...how close were Abby and Rob?

"Do you think she was unhappy?" I asked quietly. "You were in some of her classes; did the teachers give her a hard time?"

"No," Sarah said, sounding surprised. "She always seemed to get on well with them...and with everyone. Though, I did notice that she was kind of..." She paused, as though searching for the right words.

"What?" I prompted, desperate for an insight.

"I don't know. I remember thinking she seemed a bit distracted sometimes, like she was daydreaming in class and sitting with her friends, without really interacting...but I might just have imagined it."

I tried to picture Abby with her friends, in the canteen at lunch, in class... I realised I hadn't taken much notice of what she got up to at school. "I reckon she was totally seduced by the Barn."

"And Rob?" Sarah said.

I pursed my lips. "Probably."

We climbed into the back of Callum's car, Jill claiming the passenger seat. Callum shot me a brief look of panic through the mirror as she chattered on about music, listing all of the gigs she'd been at in the last year. I smiled.

"So are you reading any poetry tonight, Callum?" Sarah asked when Jill took a breath.

"No; a couple of friends probably will. I don't think they're any good though."

"How's Tom doing?" I asked.

"Okay." Callum nodded. "He won't talk much about anything though. I'm still not sure if these guys have bothered him before, though he did tell me they're in his year."

"What happened?" Sarah asked.

"Tom just ran into some trouble yesterday," I said, not knowing how much Callum would want to reveal.

"We can keep an eye out for him in school if he's getting hassle," Jill said.

"Thanks, Jill," Callum said. "You'd probably get on well with him actually. Some of those bands you were talking about, he's into as well. Though he keeps listening to that Relapse lately."

"Rob's band?" I asked.

"Yeah." Callum made a face. "They apparently handed out limited edition EPs to some folk and Tom got his hands on one."

"Are they signed?" Jill asked.

"Doubt it," Callum said. "I think they just play gigs at the Barn."

"I thought they sounded good," Jill said.

Sarah focused her attention on me, but I didn't say anything, gazing out the window to avoid her scrutinising gaze. Sarah was too inquisitive sometimes and good at guessing what I was thinking. I didn't like her questioning what Rob was to me, as I was still trying to figure that out myself.

We arrived at the university car park. Callum parked his car and we walked down to the Union, Jill hardly able to contain her excitement. She was practically skipping down the hill. I envied her enthusiasm; I couldn't remember what excitement felt like.

"Do you guys have fake ID?" Callum asked.

I nodded. "We got some made last year for an over-eighteens gig."

"Cool, they probably won't ask, but just in case." He walked up to the main doors and held them open.

We walked into a darkened corridor and two students sat at a desk, one of them holding a clipboard. He slid it towards Callum, who flashed him his student card. "I'm signing in these three."

The students glanced at us then nodded, resuming their conversation. Jill nipped my arm. "We must look eighteen, cool eh?" she hissed in my ear.

We followed Callum into a room set out with rounded tables, a dimly lit stage to one side of the bar. Students sat in groups, laughing and talking. I was surprised and a little disappointed by how young and...ordinary...they looked. It didn't quite match the images of hip eclectics I'd been carrying around in my head.

Callum led us to a table near the stage, where two boys and a girl sat. They waved as he approached, surveying us curiously.

Callum pulled over some extra seats for us and we sat down. Sarah looked nervous and Jill was staring at the girl, no doubt wondering if she was competition.

"This is Kat and her friends, Sarah and Jill," Callum said. "This is Joe, Henry and Olivia."

We all said our hellos. Olivia smiled at me, then shot Callum an eyebrow raise and I wondered what that was all about.

Henry sat mumbling under his breath, glancing down at a sheet of paper in front of him.

"He's up first tonight," Joe explained to me.

"Right." I glanced down at the paper. "What's your poem about, Henry?"

Henry closed his eyes, muttering one last word then turned his attention to me. "Death."

Jill and Sarah exchanged uncomfortable glances.

"Cheery subject," I said. Callum shot me a concerned look. I wanted to tell them all to relax.

"Henry is a cheery guy," Olivia said sarcastically, sipping her beer.

"Want to help me get drinks?" Callum stood up, looking over at me.

"Sure." I turned to Jill and Sarah. "What d'you want, guys?"

"Just a Coke," Sarah said quietly.

"G and T," Jill said.

I followed Callum to the bar, watching as a plump woman adjusted a microphone on stage. A light flicked on above her and the noise of the crowd died down as she introduced the night.

"We have a number of Riverside University students taking the stage tonight, along with some guests from the City Art School doing a music and spoken word collaboration..."

My heart kicked against my chest. There were hundreds of students at City Art School. He wouldn't be here...I quickly scanned the room as Callum ordered the drinks.

"Your friend Jill talks a lot," Callum said.

"Yeah, sorry," I said. "I think she likes you."

"Oh? You been telling her good things about me?"

"Of course." I smiled.

"She's a cool girl," he said. "But not really my type." He shot me a pointed look and I averted my gaze. Maybe Sarah had been right, that he *had* hoped to get me alone tonight. The idea panicked me; Callum was *nice*, but like a brother kind of nice...

"Cool place," I said, changing the subject. "D'you come here a lot?"

"Sometimes after lectures and on the weekends." He gestured to the stage. "There's Henry."

Henry walked across the stage, a sombre expression on his face. He adjusted the microphone and closed his eyes, standing in silence. Then suddenly his eyes flew open and he launched into his poem.

"DEATH. Like a raven, spreading its wings of doom over me, across me, pecking at me. Listen, listen, LISTEN..."

I suppressed a laugh and Callum smirked. "He's a tad intense," he whispered in my ear. We picked up the drinks and walked back to the table. I noticed another girl had joined us. She was watching Henry, a frown on her face.

"It's bad taste," she was saying to Olivia. "It's not what this town wants to hear about just now."

I sat down beside her and a flicker of surprise crossed her face as she glanced at me.

"Oh, you're Kat Sullivan," she said.

"Yeah," I replied, trying to place her face.

"Sorry," she said. "You don't know me. I just recognise you... from the papers..."

"Oh." I took a swig of my drink, turning my attention back to Henry, not wanting to answer any questions she might have.

"...it is sucking the life from me, taking me to dark places, I can hear it calling me...listen, listen, LISTEN..."

"I know what you must be going through," she said, lowering her voice so that only I could hear. "My wee cousin, Sophie...she was one of them..."

"The suicides?" I said stupidly. What else would she have meant.

She nodded. "It was horrific, still is horrific. Not having any answers. My aunt and uncle ended up moving away."

My mind ran over the newspaper clippings I'd collected about the suicides. Sophie...She had been found hanging from a tree in the woods a few weeks before Abby. Another pretty girl, seemingly happy, with everything in life to look forward to.

"Are the police still investigating? Have they found anything?" she asked.

I shook my head. "They've come up with nothing."

"What about you?"

"I'm drawing blanks too."

"Sorry, tell me to shut up if you don't want to talk about it," she said. "I'm Heather by the way."

"It's okay," I said. "Were you close to Sophie?"

She shrugged. "I saw her quite a bit. She was so smart and planned to go to uni. It's so sad that she just threw it all away. I just don't get it."

"Me neither," I mumbled.

"Did your sister go to that Barn place?" Heather asked.

My heart quickened. I nodded. "Did Sophie?"

"One of her friends told me that she'd started to go there a lot."

A strange sensation washed over me, like icy fingers creeping up my spine.

"I went to check it out a few times. It's kind of a weird place," Heather said.

"Did you ever mention it to her parents?"

Heather shook her head. "Her friends asked me not to. It seemed harmless enough; better they're all in there together than hanging around drinking on street corners where the gangs are. Don't you think?"

"I guess so," I said. "Did her parents search through her computer and stuff? Did she keep a diary?"

"No...that was another weird thing that happened..." Heather sat forward. "Her laptop and mobile phone went missing. They were never found."

I shivered. "Like someone took them?"

Heather shrugged. "Or maybe she got rid of them for some reason."

"Everything okay?" Sarah whispered at my other side. "You look a bit freaked."

"I'm fine," I said quickly. My brain was beginning to fog. Abby never used a computer; she borrowed my laptop from time to time and searching through the history of that hadn't revealed anything significant. She'd bought a new mobile a few days before her death so there was hardly anything on it and no one knew what she'd done with the old one. It had struck me as strange that she'd got a new one, when she must have known she wouldn't need it for much longer. But her journal...that would reveal clues. Just like Sophie's laptop and phone.

I turned back to Heather. "Was Sophie buried?"

She frowned. "She was actually. Why d'you ask?"

"D'you know if that was something she had talked about...or was it her parents' decision?"

Heather looked at me strangely. "I'm not sure."

I had an overwhelming desire to speak to the relatives of all of the victims, to ask them if these were common factors...missing belongings, burials...pain, memories...it wasn't something they would probably want to talk about. But surely the police would be suspicious about the missing items...

"You have got to be freaking kidding me." Callum's tone caught my attention.

I followed his gaze towards the stage and realised Henry had finished his piece and the next act was setting up. A male stepped into the light, adjusting the microphone, a guitar strung across his body. My heart leapt into my throat.

"Is he stalking you or something?" Callum shot in my direction.

Everyone at the table turned to look at me.

I laughed nervously. "Don't be ridiculous." I looked back at the stage, just to check that it was actually him. What was he doing here?

"That's Rob, right?" Sarah whispered.

I nodded. "Why would he come here?"

"Who is he?" Heather asked me.

"Just some guy," I said casually, watching as Michael sat down on a stool beside him.

"Did he know you were coming here?" Sarah mouthed to me.

I shook my head.

The room quietened as Rob strummed on his guitar and started to recite a poem, Michael accompanying him at various points.

"...our bodies merge, skin against skin, I can taste your desire, it burns, light a match, dance in fire..."

"Saucy," Jill said. "I think he's talking about sex."

"I'd have sex with him any day," Olivia mumbled under her

breath, not taking her eyes off the stage.

A loop of desire crept up my legs as I listened to his voice, as I listened to his words. A ridiculous sensation of jealousy washed over me as I wondered who he might be thinking about as he spoke…

"…fall into me, let me undress your soul, take you places untold, our desire burns, touch after touch, you unfold…"

His fingers moved slowly as he strummed the guitar, the lean muscle on his arms flexing every time he moved. His hair hung in his eyes as he looked down at each chord change.

Look up. Look at me.

And just at that moment, as the words fully formed in my mind, he did. His eyes met mine and he held my gaze until it felt like we were the only ones left in the room and his words were for me.

CHAPTER 11

After the performance they disappeared through a fire exit at the back of the room. Rob didn't even look back; just left. I stared into my drink, the conversation around me a fuzz of nondescript words, the subsequent poets on stage grey and listless. I kept glancing at the door, willing him to come back.

"You okay?" Sarah nudged me.

"Yeah," I mumbled, barely glancing at her.

"You want to go home? We could catch the bus, though Callum looks like he could easily be persuaded to hit the road."

I glanced over at Callum. He was trying to spin a peanut on the table, a scowl on his face.

"Okay," I said. We pulled our coats on and Jill made a face.

"We're not leaving already," she huffed.

"I'm sure if you wanted to stay, Callum could take you home," I said loud enough for him to hear. Jill's face brightened.

Callum jumped up, pulling his coat on. "No, no. It's late. I don't mind taking you all home."

Jill's smile slipped and I felt a pang of guilt.

"Maybe you should all stay and I can just go…" I whispered to Sarah.

"I want to go home too…and Callum clearly doesn't want to stay if you're not," she whispered back.

We all said our goodbyes.

Heather leaned forward. "Look me up on Facebook if you ever want to talk. My surname is Smith."

"Okay, thanks," I smiled.

The air was humid when we stepped outside. The ground was damp and smelled of rain, like there had been a storm while we'd been inside. A full moon shone in the sky and I stared up at it, entranced by its glow. It stirred a restless feeling inside me, evoking the desire to run away somewhere and do something reckless.

Jill turned to me. "That Rob guy is pretty intense, isn't he?"

I nodded, not wanting to discuss him with anyone, particularly not Jill.

As we headed down to the car park a scuff of trainers against gravel caused me to turn my head. Someone was leaning against a car and I squinted, trying to make out the shape. He stepped forward and the moonlight caught his face. My insides flipped.

Jill grabbed my arm so tight I had to shrug her off.

"I think he's been waiting for you," she hissed.

"Kat, we should get home." Sarah stepped forward, her brow creasing with worry.

"I'll just be a sec." I walked over to Rob slowly, assessing how he reacted. I wasn't convinced that he was waiting on me.

"I wondered how long it would take you to leave," he said, a smirk playing on his lips.

I glanced inside the car, checking he was alone. "Where's Michael?"

"He left. He's setting up a party back at the Barn. I wondered if you might like to come?"

"Well…" I glanced back at Jill and Sarah who were watching intently. "They've got school in the morning and Callum was going to take us home…"

"Not them," Rob said. "Just you."

"Oh."

His eyes burned into mine. A little thrill jolted through my body.

"I can take you home afterwards if you want. I'm not drinking."

The sensible part of my brain told me to walk away now, but a bigger part of me wanted to go with him. *Do something spontaneous for a change,* a little voice inside me whispered.

"Hang on." I walked back to Jill and Sarah. Callum was kicking stones. "If it's okay with you guys I'm going to stay...with Rob for a bit."

Jill raised an eyebrow and Sarah looked concerned. "You sure?" she asked.

I nodded.

"You alright with that, Callum? Sarah and Jill just live round the corner from you."

Callum shrugged. "Whatever. See you at work."

Sarah hugged me and whispered in my ear. "Just be careful. I'll call you tomorrow...if that's okay?"

"You never need to ask permission to call me," I whispered back.

Jill's hug was more like a throttle. "I hate you. How come you get the hotties throwing themselves at you?"

"Bye, Jill." I de-tangled myself from her grip and waved at Callum but he already had his back to me.

I walked back over to Rob, trying to appear calm and unaffected. He opened the passenger door for me and I slid inside. His car smelled of his musky aftershave and leather. I watched him walk back to the driver's side and my heart thumped in my chest. There was something really intimate about being alone with him, in a car. No escape. He climbed in beside me and started up the engine. Music clicked on.

"Placebo," I noted.

"Yeah." He fastened his seat belt and reversed the car out of the space. "You like them?"

"Prefer their older stuff. Their new stuff is too...cheerful."

He smiled. "You like your music depressing?"

"More like... soulful, or something."

"What did you think of my music when you heard us play in the Barn?"

"Relapse?" The image of him strumming on his guitar filled my mind, the hypnotic energy he had...

"Yeah."

"It was okay," I said.

"Don't go overboard there with the compliments."

"I won't," I said, glancing at his profile. My lips twitched when I noticed a smile playing on his.

"So, how long were you going to wait for me tonight? What if I'd stayed till the end?" I asked.

He stopped at traffic lights and shrugged out of his jacket. I watched as he moved, noting the black bracelet and bands tied around his wrist. He had really nice wrists, slender hands...

"I was going to give you five more minutes." He threw his jacket onto the back seats.

The lights flashed amber, green. He sped off, taking a corner too fast.

"You drive fast," I commented, adjusting my seat belt.

He grinned. "I'm just trying to unnerve you. I'm a good driver."

"Why would you want to unnerve me?" I asked.

"Because it's fun," he said. "So what were you doing there tonight? Did you know I was performing?"

"No," I said quickly. "Callum invited me along. He goes to uni there and his friend was performing."

"Callum." Rob said his name, like he was inhaling a bad smell. "He's too uptight."

I didn't say anything. Debating Callum was not something I wanted to get into.

"I didn't know you write poetry," I said, changing the subject.

"Why would you?"

"Playing in a band, writing poetry and painting, sculpting... whatever. Very creative," I said.

"There is never enough creativity, sweetheart," he said.

"I'm not your sweetheart."

He smirked. "Fine. I wasn't saying you were; it was just a term of endearment." He skipped through some songs. "Here's a nice depressing one for you..."

The chords changed to a minor key.

"What did you think of my poem?" he asked.

I squirmed, glancing at him out of the corner of my eye. His face relayed no traces of emotion; he was infuriatingly hard to read.

"It was quite...intense," I chose my words carefully.

"Did it make you blush?"

"No," I said indignantly, instantly feeling myself blush.

He chuckled.

I folded my arms and looked out the window.

"Are you mad at me now?"

"No," I said. "Why would I be?"

"Just checking." He swung the car round onto a dark road and we drove along a bumpy track.

I could see lights up ahead from the Barn.

"Who's going to be at the party?" I asked, starting to feel nervous.

"Just some friends. Private party tonight."

"D'you usually have parties on Monday nights?"

"Nah, it's Michael's birthday."

Rob swung the car into an open space in front of a wall. He switched off the engine and turned to look at me. I could almost hear my heart beating in the silence.

"Just stick by me and you'll be fine," he said. "Michael can get a bit...annoying...when he's drunk. Just ignore him."

I frowned, thinking that sounded like some kind of warning. I glanced out the window, looking up at the Barn, shadows dancing against the walls. A private party might be wilder than at the weekends. I wondered if Abby had ever been to one, and if Rob had taken her.

My phone beeped.

Rob glanced down at my bag. "That'll be lover boy checking I'm being a gentleman."

I shot him a withering look, switching off my phone without checking.

"He's right to be wary of me," he said. He looked at me out the corner of his eye.

I shivered. "What do you mean?"

"Just don't get too close to me."

"Why?" I frowned.

"I can be an arse," he said.

"Well, I already know that," I said jokingly.

A darkness fell across his face as he glanced up at the Barn. It disappeared as he turned to smile at me. "So, you ready to party?"

He was out the car before I had the chance to question him more.

CHAPTER 12

The sounds of music and laughter beckoned me to enter a different world for a while. Goosebumps prickled along my arms as Rob laid a hand casually at the base of my back and we walked round to the side entrance.

He knocked loudly on the door. It opened a slit.

"It's me, Rob," he said.

The door swung open and a girl with really long red hair jumped down off the stool and kissed him on the cheek. Her eyes were a vivid blue, almost violet, and she had green flowers painted across her sculpted cheekbones.

"Hey, Rob." She turned to me and looked me up and down. "Have a good night."

I followed Rob up the stairs, glancing over my shoulder. She was watching me, sucking on a lolly pop; probably wondering what I was doing here with him.

We walked into the crowd and this time there was an intimacy to the atmosphere, like I'd stepped into a private world where everyone spoke their own secret language. People were dancing, staring into one another's eyes, or dancing alone with their eyes closed, completely lost in the music or lost inside themselves.

A film projected onto the back wall, like the first night I'd been here. Black and white images, stills and scenes from films. Kurt Cobain sitting on a stool playing a guitar and then shots of him larking around, like footage from a behind-the-scenes documentary. Then images of River Phoenix; photographic stills.

"You want a drink?" Rob's breath was warm against my ear.

I turned away from the film. "Sure."

"What d'you fancy?"

You, a little voice inside my head whispered. "A Coke is fine."

"Okay, wait here." He patted my shoulder then disappeared into the crowd.

I turned back to watch more of the film, different scenes featuring River were now flashing up...I recognised *My Own Private Idaho.* Abby used to love his stuff, always bemoaning the fact that she hadn't been around when he was a star. She used to say it was kind of cool he got to stay twenty-three forever. A feeling of nausea settled in the pit of my stomach as I realised she now got to stay seventeen...forever.

More stills appeared...of James Dean, Marilyn Monroe, Heath Ledger, Amy Winehouse. All of them died too young...

"Kitty Kat."

Michael's face appeared in front of me.

I stepped back, startled. "Hi."

"How are you tonight?"

"Fine," I said.

He looked back at the screen. "Enjoying my little montage?"

"You seem to have a fascination with dead stars."

"They were fascinating people. All so talented, attractive, with a bit of a cult following, but also quite troubled," he said. "You have to wonder what they'd be like if they were still here today. Probably just as well they're not; beauty and talent always fades, doesn't it?"

It was a rhetorical question; he looked lost in thought and appeared to be talking to himself more than me. There was something unsettling about the intensity of his eyes, like a million emotions were darting around behind them, just waiting to tumble out unexpectedly.

"Happy birthday," I said.

He looked surprised. "Thanks. Rob told you?"

I nodded. "How old are you?"

He took out a cigarette from behind his ear and flicked a lighter. "Twenty." He took a drag of his cigarette and held it out to me.

"Want a puff?"

I shook my head.

He peered at me through crinkled eyes as he took another drag. "What do you and Rob talk about?"

I was taken aback by the question. "I don't know…stuff."

"Has he told you much about this place?"

"No, just that you use it as studios…" I said. "I know it's modelled on Andy Warhol's Factory."

"We wanted to make it a place artists and the like could hang out in. Where people get to be free to be whoever they want to be." He waved his hand. "People seem to like it, but kids can get a bit impressionable."

"What d'you mean?" I asked.

"Rob reckons we should stop letting unders in," he said. "What d'you think?"

I frowned, not sure why he was talking to me about this. "I don't know…I think we can handle it."

"Hey." Rob appeared with my drink. "What you talking about?"

A look passed between the two of them, one that I couldn't quite read.

"Stuff," Michael said.

Rob stared at Michael and I started to feel uncomfortable as he clearly wanted him to leave.

Michael half smirked then patted Rob on the shoulder. He raised an eyebrow at me. "Catch you later."

"What were you talking about?" Rob asked.

I laughed. "What is with the two of you?"

"What?" Rob frowned.

"He just asked me what *we* talk about," I said.

Rob's frown deepened. "That's none of his business. What did you tell him?"

"Nothing. He told me you wanted to stop letting unders in."

Rob took a drink of Coke, shaking his head dismissively. "It was just something I'd been thinking about."

"Why?" I asked.

"I guess when we first created this place I hadn't really thought about it attracting high school kids," he said.

"Don't you like us hanging around here?"

"You're not a high school kid any more," he reminded me.

I smiled, realising he was right. It felt freeing. No timetables to follow, no exams or essays to worry about.

"Do you dance?" he asked.

I shook my head.

"Come on, I love this song." He grabbed my hand and pulled me into the middle of the crowd. It was a song I loved too and the bass line pulsated through the soles of my boots. He started to dance, lights flashing green and blue across his face. I swayed slightly to the music, my body tense and nervous. I watched Rob as he lost himself in the beats and started to loosen up, his uninhibited movements contagious.

I glanced over his shoulder and people were laughing and smiling as they jumped around to the song. Rob grabbed my hand and twirled me around and a surge of happiness hit me hard, unexpectedly. I laughed as I spun and the room spun with me, a merry-go-round of colours and faces and lights and music and noise.

He started to sing lyrics of the song to me and his face was close to mine. My brain was disconnecting, my heart pumping all thoughts into oblivion.

"You're really beautiful," he whispered in my ear. I stepped closer to him and his arm wound around my waist. Leaning my head against his shoulder I closed my eyes, feeling the music moving through me, feeling beautiful... feeling happy. I had forgotten what happy was.

His body suddenly tensed and he stepped back. I opened my eyes in surprise.

"What is it?" I asked.

"Nothing," he said. His Adam's apple bobbed up and down as he swallowed. He took another step away from me.

A pain prickled under my skin, of humiliation and confusion. I turned away from him.

"I'm sorry." He touched my arm.

"No you're not," I said, my eyes burning. "You already told me. You don't get attached to anyone and you're an arse."

"Right." He hesitated. "There's something about you..."

"What?"

He moved closer again. "There's something about you that is making me go a little bit nuts."

The room spun, like I was moving and everyone else was standing still. It was disorientating. "Did you say the same thing to my sister?"

Confusion flickered across his face. "What?"

"Did you make Abby fall in love with you?" I said, the bitterness in my voice taking me by surprise.

"I don't *make* anyone fall in love with me."

"What, it just *happens*?"

My hands were shaking and I gripped my bottle of Coke tighter, scared that I would drop it.

"Are you saying that you're in love with me?" he whispered in my ear.

"I need to pee," I said, starting to walk away. I turned back, realising I had no idea if they even had toilets.

"Toilet is that way." He pointed in the direction of a door with a green hand on the front. He took my bottle of Coke from me to hold.

"Thanks," I mumbled, weaving through the crowds. A boy with no top on and a bandana tied around his head stepped in front of me, grinning and dancing. I moved to the side and he stepped with me, trying to entice me to dance with him.

"Excuse me." I ducked past him and he shrugged, moving on. I pushed the toilet door open and flicked on a light. There was a sink in the corner and a mirror with silver stars painted around the edges. I walked through another door to the toilet and shut it, locking it. I shut my eyes and leaned back against the door, my head spinning, emotions darting around my body. He was so infuriating. Why couldn't I just walk away? Tell him to get lost. Every time I was around him I felt this *pull*. I'd never felt so drawn to anyone, and so wanted. But then an image of Abby flashed into my mind, imagining her here with him, like this. She must have felt the same…and me being with him felt like such a betrayal.

The music thumped through the floor, through the soles of my boots. Faint voices floated through the vent above the toilet. After flushing, I put the lid down and climbed up unsteadily, placing my ear closer to the vent, catching snippets of conversation.

"…don't want anyone hanging around in here…"

"We're just wanting to see the tribute to them…"

"…some of the kids watch it when they're here…"

"…stays off limits. I don't want people seeing my degree stuff…"

I held my breath, straining to hear more but the voices faded and then a door slammed.

I jumped down from the toilet and went out to the sink, glancing in the mirror as I washed my hands. My pupils were dilated and cheeks flushed. I looked free, alive…

The door opened and a girl with short spiky hair walked in. "Alright?" she greeted me, smiling. Her eyes were unfocused. "Like the new hair, Abby. Suits you." She walked into the toilet and didn't bother to shut the door.

I glanced back in the mirror, feeling sick.

I walked back out into the Barn, tying to see what was next to the toilet; a door with a faded image of Marilyn Monroe on it. Checking no one was watching, I tried the handle; it didn't budge.

"Everything okay?" Rob appeared at my side.

"Yeah." I turned away from the door, making a mental note to try to get in there sometime. "Take me home, will you?"

"I thought you'd never ask," he said, grinning.

"You are exhausting," I spluttered.

"Why?"

"Because one minute you're all intense and acting like you're into me...then you're all arrogant and acting like a twelve-year-old."

"Okay, I'll take you home." He laid a hand on my elbow and steered me through the crowds. "You sound like you're about to have a stroke."

I hurried down the stairs; his steps behind me slow and leisurely. The girl with red hair was still sitting on the stool. She shot me a curious look as I lifted the bolt of the door and stepped outside.

A fork of lightning flashed across the skies, followed minutes later by a rumble of thunder. I loved storms and tonight it was especially fitting for my mood.

Rob unlocked the car and we got in. I kept my eyes fixed on the window so I didn't have to look at him.

"Let's get you home then," he said, pushing his foot flat to the ground so we sped down the track.

I mumbled directions.

"I know where you live," he said casually.

"How?"

"I walked Abby home one night when she got a bit drunk."

I searched my mind for memories of Abby arriving home drunk. I couldn't even remember her ever coming home late.

"She climbed in her window. Handy having a tree outside," he smiled, like he had read my mind.

"She climbed the tree?" I said in disbelief.

"Yeah," he said.

Images of her climbing a different tree filled my head and I tried to block them out. Was that what gave her the idea, knowing that she had successfully climbed one before? Except the tree in Eddison Woods took her away, rather than bringing her home.

"I can't believe I didn't know that," I mumbled.

"I don't think she was in the habit of doing things like that," he said, like he wanted to reassure me. "And she didn't usually get that drunk either."

"Such the gentleman walking her home," I said, surly, not liking the image of him escorting my sister home in a drunken state. Did she try to kiss him...did he try to kiss her?

"I'm a gentleman..." he said. "When I want to be."

We drove the rest of the way in silence. Another roll of thunder rippled the skies; this time there was no lightning.

Rob slowed down as we approached my house. All of the lights were on.

"Oh great," I glanced at the clock on his dashboard. One a.m. Mum and Dad would be livid. "Stop a bit before the house, would you?"

Rob slammed on the breaks. "You going to be in trouble?"

I shrugged. "I didn't think they'd notice."

"Good luck." He shot me a wry smile.

"Any advice? What did you used to tell your parents when you rolled in late?"

"My parents died when I was thirteen."

"Oh." A horrible feeling dragged at my insides. "Sorry."

"Don't be." He smiled tightly. He nodded to my house. "You'd better get inside. They'll be worried."

"Yeah." I nodded. "Thanks for bringing me home."

"Pleasure," he said.

I stepped out the car and took my time walking up the path to the house. I turned back and watched Rob speed back up the street, disappointed that he hadn't even said goodbye or talked about seeing me again.

CHAPTER 13

The house was eerily quiet when I walked inside, the ticking of the clock in the hallway pointed and exaggerated.

"Hello?" I called, shrugging my jacket off and clinging onto it, like it was a protective barrier.

The living room door opened and I sucked in my breath as Dad walked out, followed by Mum. Their faces were tired and drawn and I could tell Mum had been crying. Guilt and panic gripped at my bones simultaneously.

"I'm sorry, I should have called. I thought you would have gone to bed, wouldn't notice..." The excuses tumbled out.

"Where have you been?" Dad asked quietly.

"I was at a poetry thing, with Sarah and Jill..."

"We called Sarah two hours ago," Mum said. "She told us you left with a friend. What friend? And why was your phone switched off?" Her voice had traces of hysteria.

I touched my bag, forgetting that I'd switched my phone off in Rob's car. "It's just some guy I know...sorry I didn't realise my phone was off."

"What guy?" Dad asked. "Where were you all this time?"

"He's just some guy. I was at a party," I mumbled.

"On a Monday night?" Mum raised her voice. "Do you have any idea how worried we were? What thoughts were going through our heads? You DO NOT go to parties with strange boys without telling us. You DO NOT stay out till one a.m. We were just about to phone the police..."

"I'm sorry," I said. "I didn't think."

"You should have," Dad said, his voice dripping with such disappointment I wanted to sink into the carpet. "After everything...

that's happened. We need to know where you are."

"Then try talking to me once in a while," I shouted, my anger surprising me.

They recoiled, like I'd slapped them across the face.

"What does that mean?" Mum asked quietly.

I sighed. "I'm tired. Can we talk about this tomorrow?"

"You think we've not been talking to you enough?" she asked. "You think that gives you the right to sneak out till all hours with god knows who, doing god knows what?"

"You want to know what I was doing?" I raised my voice. "I was having fun. Something of a rarity these days. Maybe you should try it sometime." I stomped up the stairs, my anger fuelling every step, building and building. "And don't you dare make me feel guilty about feeling happy. I'm entitled to have some fun."

"Get back down here right now, Katrina. We've not finished talking to you yet," Dad shouted after me.

"I'm done talking," I shouted back.

"Well, you're grounded for a month, young lady. Work and back home...that is it," Mum shouted.

"Fine." I slammed my room door shut and kicked off my boots, climbing into bed fully clothed. My body shuddered with anger and unshed tears. How pathetic, grounding me like I was some stupid twelve-year-old. It was laughable. I curled up into a ball, resting my chin on my knees. My breathing subsided as my anger died down.

They would have been worried...of course I should have called. I had never in my life stayed out until after midnight, unless I was sleeping over at Sarah's. But I was seventeen, not a kid. And I had a right to be angry with them; they barely talked to me, made me feel like I had to walk around on eggshells all the time. Being with Rob tonight had made me feel alive inside...like I could do anything...

Rob. How would I be able to see him, now I'd been grounded? I closed my eyes, the image of him playing his guitar imprinted on my brain. Dancing with me, telling me I was beautiful…the way it felt, resting my head on his chest…telling me I was driving him nuts. I smiled. A shiver of excitement ran through my body. Then I remembered his other words, the warning; *Don't get too close to me.*

"Why not, Rob?" I whispered to the darkness. "Why not?"

The next morning I got up to find a note pinned to the fridge.

Phoned Mrs Hodge first thing and have written all of your work shifts into the kitchen calendar for the rest of the week so we know when to expect you home. We'll see you for dinner tonight to talk. Have a good day. We love you.

I re-read the last line. My parents were never very demonstrative with their emotions. Mum's words stirred a strange mix; of anger that they wanted to keep a close track on me…but at the same time a warm feeling, that they loved me, that they wanted to keep me safe. Had Abby felt like they didn't care? Like I didn't care? I tried to remember if I'd ever told her I loved her.

The phone rang. I glanced at the clock, wondering who would be calling. It was nine a.m. Probably Mum checking that I was up. I laid down my half-eaten cereal and picked up the phone.

"Hello?"

I could hear someone breathing on the other end.

"Hello?" I repeated.

"Is Abby there?"

It was a male voice, muffled and gruff, like they were half covering the receiver.

"Who is this?" I demanded.

"Someone who knew her," the voice said.

"You're speaking in the past tense. So you must know she's dead, you sick freak. Why are you phoning here, asking for her?"

My hands shook with anger.

"Don't you miss her? Don't you wish you could be with her? I bet she's having much more fun, on the other side..."

I slammed the phone down, tears stinging my eyes. Who would do that? I punched in 1471. Number withheld again. I opened the drawer where we kept takeaway numbers, business cards...looking for the card a sympathetic police officer had given us...Yvonne. She'd said we could call anytime. I pulled out the card and dialled her number, my palms sweating against the receiver.

"Good morning, Yvonne Bishop how may I..."

"Hi, it's Kat...Kat Sullivan." I cut her off before she'd finished her introduction.

There was a surprised pause. "Kat, hello. How can I help you?"

"Some sick guy keeps phoning our house asking for Abby..."

"Is it someone you know?"

"No, well I don't know." The voice hadn't seemed familiar, but it was so muffled it was hard to tell. "He knows she's dead...but he's asking for her. He asked me if I missed her, taunting me."

"I'm sorry, that must have been upsetting for you. When did he phone?"

"Just there. He phoned the other night too, at dinner...my Mum answered."

"Have you been able to trace a number?"

"No, both times number withheld."

"Are your parents there just now?"

"They're at work."

"D'you want me to come over?"

"No, I'm fine...I have to go to work too in a minute. I just wondered if you could trace the call?"

"If you give me details of your telephone provider we can get in touch with them."

After giving her details my mind returned to the conversation I'd had with Heather last night about her cousin Sophie. "There was something else I wanted to talk to you about..."

"Go ahead," Yvonne said, her voice calm and reassuring.

I told her about Sophie's missing belongings, reminded her about Abby's missing journal. "I just wondered if the others...if their things were missing too."

There was silence on the other end. A suspicious silence like Yvonne was trying to figure out what she should...could?..say to me.

"I'm not really at liberty to discuss much about the other... suicides...but we are aware of some missing belongings," she said.

"Don't you think that's weird?" I said. "Why would their things go missing? It's like someone took them, like someone else was involved in all of this."

"We've been considering they may have made some kind of suicide pact with one another..." Yvonne said quietly.

I frowned at the phone.

"...And they didn't want anyone to know...because maybe there're others who were or are still involved. There's not much we can do in clear cut...suicides...such as this, Kat, but do tell us of anything else suspicious you hear. It was good of you to phone me and tell me this today."

I shook my head, not agreeing with her theory. "But Abby didn't even know the others that well. She was sort of friends with some of them, but not close. She wouldn't have made a pact with them..."

"I'm not saying she definitely did. But it would be one explanation for why their things disappeared and why they all chose the same location and method of suicide. I know it's frustrating not having answers, Kat. It's frustrating for us also, trust me."

My head was spinning. A suicide pact. It hadn't even crossed my mind. But it just didn't seem likely.

"We'll get back to you about the phone calls," Yvonne said, obviously trying to bring our conversation to a close.

"Okay, thanks." I hung up and headed to work.

Unanswered questions tumbled through my head as I walked through the streets. Nothing made sense. It was exhausting and part of me just wanted to forget, just accept Abby was gone...it was the only way to let go, to start moving on.

As I passed the park I noticed a boy in school uniform sitting on the swings, smoking.

He looked up when I stopped at the gate.

"Tom," I said, surprised.

He threw his cigarette on the ground, stubbing it out with his trainer.

I smiled. "It's okay." I gestured to the cigarette. "I won't tell your brother."

He took a headphone out of one ear. "I don't care if you do."

I sat down on the swing beside him. He stared at his feet, clearly uncomfortable.

"How come you're not in school?"

He shrugged. "Didn't feel like it."

There was still some bruising around his eye, giving him an air of vulnerability.

"School can be shit sometimes. D'you miss your old friends?" I asked.

He shrugged again. "Sometimes," he mumbled.

"I would've hated it if my parents had moved when I was going into fifth year. Just when you want to start going to parties and stuff and you suddenly don't know anyone."

His shoulders relaxed a bit and he pushed his hair back from his eyes. He was striking; clear blue eyes like Callum but a much more feminine, structured face. "I go to parties at the Barn. The guys there are cool."

"Yeah, I remember seeing you there," I said.

"I don't really have much in common with a lot of people in my year," he said.

"Who do you talk to in the Barn?" I asked.

"Rob and Michael." He paused, blushing slightly. "And Chloe..."

I smiled. *Chloe*. Hmm.

"Are you Rob's girlfriend?" He looked at me curiously and I felt a little thrill that he would think that.

"No," I said. "We're just...friends." Were we even friends?

"Do you miss your sister?" he asked quietly.

I was taken aback by him asking such a personal question. "Yeah, every day."

"I've seen pictures of her at the Barn. She looked like a cool person."

An image of Abby, smiling and running towards me filled my mind. "She was."

"I don't think she'd want you to be sad," he said, in a knowing way.

I frowned, thinking that was such a strange thing for someone who'd never met her to come out with. "Why d'you say that?"

"I've seen the film they were all in...like they wanted to be remembered as something other than just who they were. Like they were too beautiful and interesting to be contained here, in boring little Eddison."

Dizziness washed over me, like I was having an out-of-body experience. "What film?" My mind was whirring quick speed... pulling out memories of an overheard conversation, *We're just wanting to see the tribute to them...some of the kids watch it when they're here.*

Tom's face paled. "I shouldn't have said anything." He stood up, grabbing his backpack. "I thought you would have seen it..."

"Where did you watch it?"

"In the Barn."

"In the room with Marilyn Monroe on the door?"

He started to back away as I edged closer towards him. He looked nervous, like I was an animal getting ready to pounce on him.

"I think so...I don't really remember..." he muttered.

"Who showed it to you?" I asked.

"Michael." He pulled the straps of his backpack tight around his shoulders. "I should probably get to school now..."

"Who's in the film? What's it about?" I stepped forward as he stepped back. "Tom, *please*."

"It's just a mishmash of stuff...I didn't see the whole thing. Abby was in it and another girl, Sophie...and some guys. They're all being interviewed, philosophising about life."

"How did you get to see it? Was the room just open?" I asked.

He frowned, like he was thinking, trying to remember. "No, I remember Michael approaching some of us, me, Chloe and another couple of people from our school. He said he liked to make documentary-style films and showed us this one. He said he thought we had star quality and wanted us to be in one. I think it's for part of his art-degree show."

"And have you been in one?" I asked, wondering what the hell Michael was up to.

Tom shook his head. "I hated being in front of the camera. And I've not been back in a while...you know, since I'm grounded."

I pursed my lips, remembering my own grounding. I needed to get to the Barn, to see that film...how could I do that when I was going to be under twenty-four- seven surveillance?

"I really should go now," he said.

"Yeah, sure," I said, absentmindedly.

He started to walk away, then looked back over his shoulder.

"Don't tell Michael I told you," he said. "I think he wanted us to keep it quiet...you know, in case the police get hold of it."

I smiled grimly. "Okay, sure."

"Thanks. See you." He waved then hurried through the park.

I kicked at the wood chips under the swings. Had all of them been in his film...films even? What did that mean? That they *were* closer friends than I'd thought...and then did make some weird suicide pact?

I pulled out my mobile and keyed in Cake Tin's number.

Mrs Hodge answered on the second ring. I was relieved it wasn't Callum – he would never buy my excuses.

"Hi, Mrs Hodge, it's Kat," I said, trying to make my voice sound hoarse. "I'm really sorry but I can't come in today…I've got a really sore throat."

"I see, probably because you were out till all hours, hmm?" she said. "Does your Mum know you're not coming in today? She's asked me to keep an eye out for you."

Great. I rolled my eyes. "I'll call her to let her know, Mrs Hodge." I faked a cough. "I have to go…sorry again."

I hung up before she had the chance to say anything else. I scrolled down my phone, searching for Mum's work number then decided with her keen ears there was the danger she would detect outside noises…and Mrs Hodge might be calling her just now then she'd phone me on the house phone to check how I was. I started to run home, deciding it would be best to call from there. Then I would head to the Barn. I had to find that film.

CHAPTER 14

The rain lashed down as I pounded on the door of the Barn. I pulled my jacket tighter around me, conscious that my hair was turning into rat tails. What if no one was here? I knocked again, glancing up at the building, wondering if there was any way I could climb up onto the roof and sneak in a skylight or something.

The door flew open and I stepped back, startled.

Michael peered out at me; his hair was sticking up and there were dark shadows under his eyes. "Rob's not here..." he said, starting to shut the door in my face.

I caught it with my hand. "I'm not here to see Rob."

A flicker of surprise crossed his face, then amusement. He stepped aside. "You'd better come in. It's a bit wet out there."

I stepped inside, grateful to escape from the downpour. A shiver ran through my body.

"Come upstairs and we'll get you out of those wet clothes," he said, his eyes running up and down my body.

"I'll be fine," I said tersely, following him up the stairs. I noticed there was fresh-looking mud on his boots. That struck me as strange as he appeared to have just woken up.

He chuckled. "You're pretty uptight, Kitty Kat." He yawned, rubbing at his eyes.

Upstairs the lights were low, with a few soft lamps lit in the corners. It gave the place an eerie glow. People were sleeping on the sofas, half naked. I averted my eyes. As we walked across the room my feet crunched on discarded plastic cups and food. Empty beer bottles were piled up on the tables beside the sofas, ash trays overflowing.

"Bit messy after last night," Michael said. "Come on in to my little office. I need a coffee." He led me in the direction of a door in the far corner of the room, beside the piano. On our way past the Marilyn Monroe door I hesitated.

"What's in here?" I stopped at the door.

Michael turned and looked at me curiously. "Why do you want to know?"

I shrugged. "I like Marilyn Monroe."

He looked sceptical. "You look more like a Marilyn Manson fan to me."

I was determined to get more information out of him. "So, is there some memorabilia or something in there?"

"That's my multi-media room. I keep my film equipment in there. I do a lot of films for my Visual Communication course."

"I'm interested in film too. Can I take a look?" I tried the handle. Still locked.

"Maybe later," he said tightly. "I need coffee."

I reluctantly followed him in to his 'office'. It was a small room with a desk in the corner, notebooks spread across it, drawing pencils and pens, and a kettle and some mugs. A futon sat against the back wall, a rumpled blanket hanging off it suggesting Michael had slept there last night.

Michael clicked on the kettle and started to spoon coffee into one of the mugs. "You want some?"

"No." I shook my head, glancing up at the bookcases that lined the walls. There were lots of psychology books, biographies of Andy Warhol, Kurt Cobain, art books on Dali, Cubism and poetry books of Keats and Shelley.

"So, what's your fascination with Andy Warhol?" I asked, pulling down one of the books, taking in the black and white image on the cover, Warhol's hair standing on end like a mad professor's.

"I like how his work reflected the way culture was changing around that time. Like he totally became a part of the consumerism and depthlessness that was emerging in society." Michael stirred some sugar into his coffee. "And the way he became a celebrity. I think it's fascinating that people appeared to want to consume *him*, not just his art. He was such a weird, awkward character and yet he had all of these cool people wanting to be a part of his world... he constructed this whole glamorous life for himself."

I looked at Michael, wondering if that was what he wanted, to have cool kids wanting to be part of his life, look up to him as some kind of *icon*.

"But it's Rob who really knows more about him," Michael said, turning to face me. He rested against the desk. "Those Andy Warhol books belong to him. I think he identifies with the little boy lost in him."

I looked at him curiously. "What d'you mean?"

"Rob has always been a bit of a lost soul. When his parents died my family took him in," he said.

I blinked in surprise. "You've known Rob since you were young?"

"I guess you could say we're like brothers," he said, peering at me over the rim of his coffee mug. "I thought Rob would have told you a bit about himself by now. He's usually not slow in telling the ladies his sad little life story."

I averted my eyes, sensing that Michael was trying to rile me in some way.

"You should read the book. Take it," he said.

I hesitated, then slipped it in my bag. "Thanks."

"You struck me as a woman on a mission when I opened the door to you...what do you want?" he asked.

Okay, straight to the point. That was the way I should play it too. Standing up straighter, I hoped I could fool my body into feeling imposing and confident. "I want to see the film you made; the one with Abby in it."

There was a subtle change in his expression; he too, like Rob, was good at hiding his emotions but he had expressive eyes that had traces of worry. His knuckles whitened as he gripped his mug tighter.

"Did Rob tell you about it?"

I shook my head. "No."

He frowned. "Who?"

"Why does that matter?" I asked. I folded my arms. "I want to see it."

I could hear the sounds of people moving around outside, shoes clip clipping along the wooden flooring. Michael looked deep in thought, like he was weighing up a few things in his head.

"I'm not sure I still have it. I'll need some time to look for it," he said and I knew he was lying.

"Why don't we have a look in your multi-media room?" I pressed.

A smirk played on his lips. "You're quite determined aren't you?"

I looked him straight in the eye, answering firmly. "Yes."

He traced a finger round the rim of his coffee mug. "Abby used to talk about you quite a bit."

I didn't react, conscious that he was changing the subject.

"She didn't like being a twin," he said, watching me intently as he spoke, like he wanted to gauge my reaction.

"I didn't either."

"Really?"

"People automatically make…made…comparisons," I said carefully, not wanting to divulge much of my inner thoughts to him.

"Abby thought you were much more confident and smarter than her," he said.

I tried to keep my face non-reactive. Was he lying? Abby was always so much more confident than me; she knew I hated being in large groups, hated making conversation with people I didn't know…

"She talked about how you always stayed calm, so unaffected by everyone else, never giving a shit. She said you used to be really close but when you turned fifteen you dyed your hair black and started dressing really differently. At first she was pleased, like you were both forging out different identities, but then she began to feel a bit lost, like she'd lost a part of herself," he said, his eyes boring into mine.

I listened to his words, picturing Abby speaking to him, telling him things she should have spoken to me about. I felt the compulsion to defend myself to him, to explain it wasn't like that... but something stopped me. A little voice inside told me to keep quiet. And another voice was telling me I'd been a bad sister, that I had made Abby feel rejected. A wave of guilt flashed through me, firing the pain I already felt every time I questioned if I could have done more.

"She thought you acted superior, like you suddenly found everything she did childish, that you thought her friends were, what was it she said...?" He paused, looking away, searching for memories. "Oh yeah, 'empty heads'."

My face flushed. I remembered being annoyed one night when Abby and her friends were playing music really loud when Mum and Dad were away for the weekend and I was trying to study. I *had* called them empty heads but I hadn't really meant it. God, I did sound like such a superior bitch.

"Why would she tell you all that?" I said.

He shrugged. "I don't remember if it was me she told. It might have been Rob."

I frowned.

"Girls seem to enjoy baring their soul to him," he said casually. "And he likes to share stories with me."

Conflicting emotions stirred inside me. A mixture of confusion, anger...but deep down disbelief. Rob might be arrogant and evasive but I couldn't believe him betraying Abby's confidence like that.

I studied Michael, trying to figure him out. Then I remembered his words the previous night, asking what Rob and I talked about, and Rob's reaction to that: *"That's none of his business."* It didn't add up.

"Abby was really sweet and impressionable," Michael said. "You strike me as less so."

"You don't know me," I said.

He laid down his coffee and picked up a pack of cigarettes. He took his time sliding one out and reached into his back pocket for a lighter. "Abby liked coming here to escape. What d'you reckon she wanted to escape from?"

"I really don't know," I said, suddenly feeling exhausted.

He lit his cigarette and blew a spiral of smoke up into the air. "It's hard being seventeen. The feeling that every detail of the day is so devastatingly important that if you make one wrong move it will somehow irrevocably affect the rest of your life.

"It's sometimes hard to see the bigger picture," he continued. "Especially in a town as small as Eddison." He flashed a smile at me. "That was me quoting Abby. I just remembered lines from that film you were talking about."

He was playing with me. I glared at him. "I'd rather see the film than have you paraphrase."

He raised an eyebrow. "And I'll be happy to show it to you, Kitty Kat...just as soon as I remember where I put it." He glanced at his watch. "I have to head into art school."

"Can't we have a quick look just now?" I asked, wondering how I was going to be able to get out the house again.

"Give me a couple of days," he said. He stubbed out his cigarette on the desk and opened a drawer, rummaging around. "I've got something else to give you just now."

I waited, curious to see what he was going to pull out the drawer.

He handed me a CD. Relapse was written in blue across the front, reflected in a painting of a mirror.

"It's our EP. You should take a listen. Abby loved it. Particularly track number four." He smiled.

There was something unsettling about that smile. I shivered, then took the CD from him and slipped it into my bag.

"I really need to get going," he said, grabbing a bag from under the desk. "I'll walk you out."

Reluctantly I followed him out of the office, glancing longingly at the locked 'media room' as we walked past. I wondered if Rob would be able to let me in some time.

"Is Rob going to be at the Barn later?" I asked, trying to sound casual.

Michael shook his head. "Doubt it. He said something about working late at the art school on some project that's due. I don't think he'll be around for a couple of days."

Disappointment gnawed at me. For more reasons than I cared to acknowledge. The rain was still pounding down when we got outside.

"You want a lift somewhere?" Michael asked, holding his bag above his head.

I shook my head. "I'm fine walking."

"Okay, Kitty Kat. You enjoy the music." He shot me a grin. "And I'll tell Rob you said hi."

"Remember to look for that film," I shouted after him.

He didn't turn around but waved his hand in the air in acknowledgement.

I wouldn't let him forget.

CHAPTER 15

The rest of the week passed slowly. Mrs Hodge watched me like a hawk at work; Callum was on none of my shifts and I began to wonder if he'd requested this but couldn't bring myself to ask Mrs Hodge in case she read something into it. Mum and Dad forced me to have strained dinners with them every night; Sarah sent me regular texts, no doubt checking I wasn't about to run off into the sunset with Rob.

Rob…I was sure he would've tried to visit me at work. I tried to put him out of my mind but thoughts kept creeping back in; he was like a catchy song on a loop. A heaviness tugged at me, like a darkness was enveloping my heart.

"I'm off home now, Mrs Hodge." I grabbed my bag from the back, dying to escape.

"Okay, dear. See you tomorrow." She smiled as I walked past. "Straight home now."

"Uh huh," I sighed, wondering how the hell I was supposed to forget, seeing as this was now her regular parting shot. I fell through the door as Callum swung it open from the other side. He caught my arm as I stumbled.

"Thanks." I smiled but he didn't smile back. It threw me off guard.

"No problem," he said.

"Busy week at uni?" I asked.

"Yeah, I'm just in to check my shifts for the weekend."

"I think you're on Saturday morning. And a twelve to five with me on Monday," I said.

He nodded, looking completely uninterested.

"I got grounded after the other night," I blurted out.

"So I heard," he said. "Well, you'd better get home."

I blinked, hurt by his abruptness. "Yeah. See you." I watched as he strode to the counter and I slammed the door shut behind me, hoping he heard it. Why was he mad at me? It wasn't like we'd been on a date at the poetry reading.

I pulled my MP3 player out my bag and slid the headphones in, skipping to Relapse's EP. The music was haunting and dark, just what I felt like listening to. Rob's voice was deep and gravelly, almost hypnotic. The words of his songs had been running around my head the past few days, nearly as much as images of him. Track four was particularly dark, not Abby's taste at all; it was hard to believe this would've been her favourite song. It made me feel closer to her though; listening to it, knowing it was something she would've heard not that long ago. Maybe she would still have their EP in her room somewhere, if Dad hadn't cleared it out.

As soon as I reached home I hurried up to her room. A strange sensation washed over me as I walked inside; a feeling that someone had been there. Nothing looked out of place. I pulled out my headphones and laid down my bag, wandering around. I traced a finger along her dressing table; her jewellery box sat where I'd left it on the shelf. My eyes were drawn to the curtains which were blowing gently and I noticed the window was open slightly. I slammed it shut, my hands shaking. Had someone been here?

I turned to face the bed, my eyes distracted by a sparkle on the bedside table closest to the window. As I approached I could make out it was a notebook. That definitely hadn't been there last time.

I grabbed it, flicking through it. Pages were torn out but some still there contained more journal entries, written by Abby. Heart pounding, I looked back out the window, straining to see someone in the distance, anyone walking away along the street. The only sign of life was a cat, walking with tail held high. Someone must have climbed in her window and left the notebook there. Who...why?

The notebook shook in my hands. I sat down on the bed,

turning to the first intact page, dated

February 20th:

Things at school are getting worse. I just can't focus in class and I know my marks have slipped. I don't think I'm going to pass my final exams – my prelim results were awful, I totally lied when Mum and Dad asked me about them. What was I supposed to say with Kat rolling off her As and Bs. Sometimes I think who cares, but then wake up in a panic thinking how am I going to escape this god awful town if I don't get decent marks? I couldn't bare watching Kat swan off to uni to study Law while I'm stuck at the local college with the Neds from my year. I feel like there's this whole other life out there – like the things everyone talks about at the Barn…the life they have at art school, the travelling some of them have done…the things they know about. They know SO MUCH about such cool things, and it just makes me think there is so much more than just stupid exams. The only thing I'm remotely enjoying is Art but even that's boring me lately… I don't want to paint still lives, I want to paint REAL life. Michael thinks I should be an actress, he's told me I'm so natural on camera, like he could have imagined me being like Edie, that 'it' girl who hung around with Andy Warhol. He showed me some clips from Factory Girl the other night and she looked pretty cool, if a bit crazy. He said he wants me to be part of his Degree Show…to feature in a documentary. Me! In his film!!

I flicked forward to the next entry,

March 3rd

Rob asked if he could paint me some time. Oh my God. I cannot believe he actually wants to paint ME. He's shown me some sketches he's done of me before, like he just sits and studies me while I'm sitting talking to people in the Barn. He is so amazing, sooo gorgeous. I CANNOT stop thinking about him…Lisa reckons he fancies me. He does talk to me lots. But he talks to Sophie too. She's much prettier than me. I bet he fancies her. I know she totally fancies him; she follows him everywhere. I just feel so alive and happy :) when I'm around him!!

So she did fancy Rob. And so did Sophie. I felt sick. Her words 'so alive and happy' were like echoes of my own emotions when I was around Rob.

April 2nd

I can't believe Sophie's gone. This one has really freaked me out – I hardly knew the other suicides but being in that film with her and everything...it's just weird to think that she was really unhappy. I always thought she was so perfect, had it all. I just don't get it. Michael said that she'll always be remembered now...I'm not sure if he meant because she's on the film. It was weird watching our film again last night. She was so beautiful.

Ironic, reading Abby's words; her expressing disbelief at Sophie's suicide because she was so happy... *So were you Abby... what changed? Why just a few weeks before your own suicide are you expressing such surprise that someone could do that?* I realised with a jolt that it also meant Yvonne's theory about a suicide pact was wrong. Abby had no idea that Sophie was even contemplating killing herself.

April 11th

I think I'm in love with him. I can't sleep; I can't focus on anything else. I managed to get a copy of their EP and I just listen to it again and again, his voice is so haunting. I feel so miserable and so happy all in one. He seems to like me; I see him sitting looking at me sometimes but then he never makes a move. Maybe he thinks I'm just a dumb kid. I tried to talk to Chloe and Lisa about him but they don't get it. Well, I think Chloe does but I can tell she's jealous whenever he pays me attention and that's why she hates talking about him. I wish I could talk to Kat but she always rolls her eyes whenever I mention a guy's name. She's too busy sticking her nose in books these days anyway...working towards her dream of taking over the world or something. I was going to ask her to come to the Barn the other night but I reckon she'd tell Mum and Dad about the place. I couldn't bear not to see Rob.

The words blurred in front of me as I read the last few sentences again. Hot tears rolled down my cheeks, a tightness spreading across my chest. She felt like she couldn't talk to me. She thought I'd tell Mum and Dad about the Barn? *I wouldn't have, Abby, I would have loved it...I'm loving it. I get it.*

My thoughts were interrupted with the sound of the front door opening. I slammed the journal shut and hurried out of Abby's room into my own.

"Kat, you home?" Mum's voice floated up the stairs.

"Yeah, I'll be down in a minute," I shouted, shoving Abby's journal under my bed. I wiped at my tears and checked my reflection in the mirror, outlining my eyes with fresh liner. A big part of me wanted to talk to Mum about finding Abby's journal but then her and Dad would know about the Barn and about Rob... and about how disappointed Abby was with me. It'd make them think badly of all of us, like we were somehow to blame. Was I to blame? If only I'd talked to Abby more, encouraged her to confide in me. I was her twin for god's sake and I'd left her feeling like she couldn't even tell me she was in love.

My eyes started to sting, more tears threatening to escape.

"Kat?" Mum knocked softly on my door.

"Uh huh?" I blinked quickly and sat down on my bed, untying my boots so that I didn't have to make eye contact as she popped her head in.

"Good day at work?" she asked.

"It was okay." I shrugged.

"Yvonne from the police station called me today at lunch," she said.

My head jerked up in interest. I'd forgotten about the phone calls.

"They traced the calls to a public phone box outside Eddison Woods. There's no CCTV or anything around that part of town so there's no way of knowing who made the calls. She told us to keep a log though, in case we receive more."

I sighed. "I guess they'd have to be really stupid to phone from their own number."

Mum walked fully into my room and sat down on the bed beside me. She laid a hand on mine and I nearly flinched, I was so unaccustomed to any sign of affection from her these days.

"Are you sure you don't have any idea who could be making the calls?" she asked gently.

I shook my head. "No."

"Don't they realise how much we've already suffered?" Mum said quietly.

"They're sick."

Mum put an arm around my shoulder and squeezed me closer to her. My bottom lip trembled.

"Are you okay?" she said into my hair. "Have we let you down?"

I shook my head vigorously, tears soaking into her blouse. I clung onto her. "I think I let Abby down..."

"No." Mum stroked my hair. "Why would you think that?"

Tears prevented me from expanding and I didn't know how to answer anyway. Mum rocked me in her arms and I suddenly felt like I was six years old again; it felt comforting allowing myself to be held, not holding the pain inside alone but sharing it with someone who understood. She cried softly and I wondered if she felt relief too...in letting go.

"It's so hard not knowing," she whispered. "Sometimes I think I'm going crazy with the pain of wanting to know why."

Me too. I gripped her tighter.

"Yvonne mentioned something about them looking into it being some kind of suicide pact. I can't see Abby being involved in something like that, can you?"

"No, there's no way," I said, swallowing feelings of guilt as I thought of the answers in Abby's journal that I was keeping hidden from Mum. I just couldn't let her read it. She wouldn't understand about the Barn or Rob.

The doorbell rang and Mum pulled away from me. She took a deep breath and wiped at her face, laughing gently.

"I must look a mess," she said.

"You look fine," I said. "Want me to get it?"

"No, no." She shook her head, already heading out of the room.

I sat listening, wondering who it would be. Then I heard a familiar voice and my Mum's surprised delight. *Sarah*.

"Kat, it's Sarah," Mum shouted.

"Tell her to come up," I called back. I wiped at my face and smoothed down my hair.

My foot touched Abby's journal and I already knew Sarah would be the right person to share this secret with.

CHAPTER 16

Sarah's face paled as she read the journal entries, but showed no other reaction.

"I've only read up to the first April entry so far," I said.

Sarah pursed her lips and shut the book. She paused before looking up at me. "Who d'you think left it in her room?"

Names darted around my head but nothing made sense. "I don't know; who would have access to her journal?"

"Chloe or Lisa?" she suggested.

I shook my head. "I'm sure they would've just given it to me... why sneak it into Abby's room for me to find?"

"Maybe they were scared your parents would give them trouble for not handing it over earlier," Sarah said.

I chewed my lip. "Hmm, maybe. It just doesn't seem their style. Can you imagine either of them climbing a tree?"

Sarah appeared to share my comical visual as she laughed. Her smile faded as she seemed to be pondering other theories.

"What?" I prompted.

"I don't know...it's just weird. Like someone is trying to mess with your mind or something. Why are pages ripped out?" She flicked through the book.

"I guess there's sections this person doesn't want me to read."

"Have you found anything else?" she asked.

"I found another page under her pillow last week," I said. My eyes fell upon the painting leaning against my wall. "And this. I found this a few weeks back." I turned the painting round to show Sarah.

"It's Abby," she said quietly.

I nodded. "Rob painted it."

Her eyes darted up in surprise. "How d'you know?"

I traced a finger over his signature in the bottom corner. "I mentioned something to him about finding a painting and he said he'd done a few of her."

"Did you ask him if he happened to deliver this one in her window?" she asked dryly.

"No," I said, turning the painting back around to face the wall.

"You do realise it could be him?"

"That doesn't make any sense either. Why would he do that?"

Sarah shrugged. "To mess with your head. How much d'you really know about him? Abby writes about fancying him. She thinks that girl Sophie did too...don't you find this all a bit weird if they're all connected to the Barn...and him...in some way?"

A crashing sounded in my ears as my heart beat faster. "I doubt anyone from the Barn would want me to read this. Don't you think it's more likely to be someone who doesn't want me to go there... like they're warning me against it? And what're you saying? That Rob made them commit suicide?"

"No. Of course not," Sarah said. "It just makes me uneasy thinking about you getting involved with him."

"I'm not getting involved with him," I said. "I've not even spoken to him since the poetry reading."

Sarah fell silent. Her eyes stayed on me as I began to pace the room.

I sat down again and sighed. "I'm just so confused. I wish I could see that film that Abby was in. Maybe she says more about how she was feeling about things."

"It must be hard for you, reading her journal," Sarah said quietly.

I smiled wryly. "Especially reading the bits where I sound like a total bitch of a sister."

Sarah laid a hand on mine. "There's no way you were a bitch of a sister. And there's no way Abby would have thought that either. It's a journal where she vented about everything and anything."

"Yeah." I wasn't convinced.

"I think you should hand it in to the police," Sarah said.

I looked at her in surprise. "I can't do that."

"Why not?"

"Because then they'll tear the Barn apart, ban me...high school kids...from going. Maybe close the whole place down." I shook my head. "There's no way I could do that to Rob."

"Why? You don't owe him anything."

How could I explain to Sarah that I couldn't do this...that doing this would mean losing Rob...even if I didn't even fully have him.

"What's the attraction of this Barn place?" she asked.

I tried to think how to explain it. "It's just so...different. It's just a really cool place to hang out."

"Jill wants me to go with her tomorrow night."

A pang of jealousy hit me. "Are you going?"

"I don't know, maybe."

I could tell she had already decided she wanted to go. "Well, I'm grounded so I can't go."

"I know," she said. "It would be better if you could come too..."

I tried to ignore the stabs of misery at the thought of them getting to spend an evening with Rob while I was stuck here. "Do me a favour and remind Michael I'm still waiting to see that film."

Sarah looked a bit nervous. "What does he look like?"

"I forgot you've not met him," I said. "Tall with short black hair, really intense blue eyes. Jill should know him."

"Okay. I'll make sure I talk to him." She stood up. "I have to get home, but call me anytime if you need to."

"Thanks." I smiled.

As soon as Sarah left I picked up Abby's journal and turned to more entries.

April 21st

I've been feeling weird lately...waking up and feeling this darkness inside of me. I think Chloe and Lisa have noticed the change as they seem bored with me, like if I'm not being hyper 'happy smiley' Abby they'd rather hang out with someone else. I left school early today and spent the afternoon in the Barn. It's the only place I feel connected to these days and at least people there, like Michael, let me talk about things. I feel like he really listens to me and wants to understand. Rob wasn't there. I think there's another girl from his course who likes him; she keeps asking him to paint her but I don't think he has. The painting he did of me is hanging in the multi-media room. It's so cool. I love it. I wanted to take it home but he said he likes it in the Barn, like I add more beauty to the place.

May 7th

I feel so stupid. Oh god... I want to just hide under my covers and never come out. I got so drunk last night. Me and Rob kissed and I just melted. It was amazing. He walked me home and I told him I loved him. Stupid, stupid, STUPID. He looked totally shocked, like I'd just told him I was an alien or something. He tried to laugh it off, told me I was drunk but I kept persisting (god why could I not just shut up?) and started crying and everything. Then he told me he thought I was beautiful, that we had fun together but that was all it was. That he didn't get attached to anyone, that he didn't want a girlfriend...I'm so stupid. Now what do I do? I still love him...

I flicked through the rest of the book; the remainder an empty shell of ripped out pages and blankness. Tears ran down my cheeks. Abby had loved him and I felt her pain. "You weren't stupid. He led you on." I threw the journal across the room. He'd told me not to get too close. He needn't worry; there was no way I was going to fall in love with him.

I tried to ignore the unsettling voice that whispered somewhere deep inside, *But you already are.*

Mum and Dad asked me to join them to watch a DVD on Saturday night but I chose to retreat to my room. I turned my MP3 player up loud and tried not to picture Jill and Sarah having a great time at the Barn. And tried not to think about Rob...*tried*.

I opened my laptop and logged onto all my social media sites. I scrolled down the feeds, scanning for pictures of the Barn. It was strange how no one posted anything about it on here...then I remembered the 'Strictly No Photography' signs on the way up the stairs. Everyone seemed to respect the codes of secrecy; which in a world where everything was now totally open and in your face only added allure to the place.

I typed in a search for Rob, then realised I didn't know his surname. I scrolled through Chloe's friends looking for him or Michael...nothing. Maybe they didn't have a page? I typed in Relapse instead. My eyes were drawn to a picture of a group of five males all dressed in black. Rob stood centre stage.

I clicked on the page and noticed they had over two hundred 'likes'. They also had lots of wall posts, mainly from girls saying how great they were, lots of 'love you Rob' kiss kiss. It was nauseating. He probably loved the attention.

I moved the cursor to the pictures section. I hated myself for looking, but couldn't resist. Pictures of them all, pictures of Rob... close ups of him playing his guitar. My heart gave a little kick. I slammed the laptop shut and turned up my MP3 player even further. Would they be playing at the Barn tonight? Rob might not even be there; Michael had said he was busy with art school stuff.

I reached over and checked my phone. Eleven p.m. I wondered if Sarah would text me to let me know what was going on. Probably not. I doubted she would talk to Michael either. She'd probably be scared of him.

I pulled out my headphones and reached over to pick up the Andy Warhol book I'd borrowed from Michael, a diary-type account of life in the Factory. It was quite fascinating, reading about the characters that frequented the place and the music and fashion of the '60s. It was weird how similar the Barn was.

Tap, tap, tap.

I paused mid sentence, straining my ears to listen. Nothing. I turned back to the book, snuggling further under the covers.

Tap, tap, tap, tap.

I switched off my light and crept to the window, peeking through a gap in the curtains. Pressing my forehead close to the glass, I strained to see a dark figure step back, poised to throw a stone, his face illuminated under the streetlight outside. My heart lurched. *Rob.* He squinted up at me and waved.

I opened the window. "What're you doing here?"

He motioned for me to come down.

"No." I shook my head.

"If you don't I'll knock on the front door," he shouted back.

I knew he would. Then I'd have to explain to Mum and Dad about who he was. They'd figure out I'd been at the party with him and sparks would fly. "I'm grounded. I can't come out," I said, suddenly remembering.

"Climb out Abby's window, down the tree."

Abby's window. He'd watched her climbing in, he knew it was accessible...*was* it him leaving the things?

"Five minutes," I called, a mixture of excitement and defiance coursing through my body. I should just ignore him, go back to bed...but a bigger part of me was willing to climb anywhere just to see him again.

CHAPTER 17

With one hand I ran a brush through my hair; with the other applied mascara and eyeliner. I smudged the liner to hide the wobbly lines my shaking hand was painting. Stepping into black jeans, I pulled my nightshirt up over my head and replaced it with a black shirt. I shut my bedroom door, praying that my parents wouldn't check on me before they went to bed.

I hurried into Abby's room. Her windows were larger than mine and easy to slide up. The tree didn't look so easy to tackle. The wind rustled the leaves and I gulped as I looked down…it was quite a drop. Rob stood below, his arms folded.

"Are you coming?" he called.

"Okay, okay," I said. Tentatively I reached out to grab hold of a sturdy branch and swung one leg out the window, over onto the tree. Waves of nausea washed over me as I shakily manoeuvred my other leg out the window, grabbing onto the tree so that I was straddling the large branch.

"You want me to come up and get you?" Rob said.

"No," I snapped, shuffling my body slowly along the branch, wondering how the hell I was now going to get down. I reached up to grab hold of another branch further up and slowly stood up, taking tiny steps towards a wider middle section of the tree. I slid down to a lower branch, another lower one…then poised to jump.

"Here, I'll catch you." Rob stood below me, holding out his arms.

"Get out the way."

"Alright." He took a step back, a smirk on his face.

My breath came out in shaky gasps as I looked at the ground below. It was still a big drop. I leapt just as Rob moved back towards me. I fell into him, knocking him onto his back and landed on top of him.

"Well, hello," he said, a smile playing on his lips.

His face was dangerously close to mine. I struggled to disentangle myself, conscious that my body was making full contact with his. I pushed at him as he moved closer, then scrambled to my feet, shaking all over.

"Idiot," I said. "I told you to get out the way."

"I was just trying to help," he said, propping himself up on his elbows.

I pulled at my shirt and ran a hand through my hair.

"You look great," he said.

I folded my arms, not looking at him, refusing to acknowledge the little thrill his compliment enticed. "What d'you want?"

He jumped up. "Have I done something to make you mad?"

I tried not to breathe in his musky scent as he moved closer, tried not to look at his face, his eyes which always drew me in...

"What d'you want?" I repeated, choosing to ignore his question.

"I wanted to see you. I saw your friends at the Barn and thought you might be with them but they told me you're grounded."

My whole body tingled at the words 'wanted to see you'. *Stop it, stop it, stop it.*

"Well, here I am," I said flatly.

He frowned, his eyes searching mine. "What's up with you tonight?"

"Nothing," I said. A shiver ran through me and I pulled my arms closer around my body.

"Want my jacket?" He started to shrug it off.

"No." I shook my head.

He pulled it back on. He scratched his chin. "Okay, I'm confused. Are you still mad at me because of the other week, when I pulled away from you on the dance floor?"

"No," I said. *Yes. And because of how you made my sister feel.*

"I didn't mean to upset you. I was just...confused," he said slowly.

"Confused?"

He glanced at my house. "Can we go for a walk? Your parents might hear us talking."

"Okay. But I can't stay out long."

We headed out onto the street and I looked up at the sky, the moon a clear crescent shape glowing above us.

"Michael said you dropped by the other day," he said.

"I was asking him about a film he made. The one with Abby and Sophie...and Martin in it." I narrowed my eyes. "That day we were at the cemetery you said you couldn't remember if Martin had been at the Barn, but you must have seen that film, right?"

Rob stuck his hands in his pockets. "I've seen the film. I remember faces in it...not always so great with names. A lot of kids go to the Barn."

"And do a lot of them feature in Michael's films?" I asked.

"No." Rob shook his head. "That was one of the few he made. I think he fancies himself as a documentary film maker or something. Who told you about it?"

"That doesn't matter," I said. "I'd like to see it. D'you know if he's found it yet?"

Rob shrugged. "I can ask him for you. It might upset you watching it though."

"Why?" I asked sharply.

"Seeing Abby..."

"I need to ask you something else," I said.

"Go ahead."

"Have you been sneaking into Abby's room? Leaving stuff there?"

"What?" He stopped walking.

I searched his face for answers. He looked confused, not guilty or nervous. "Parts of her journal have started to appear."

"What do you mean...'started to appear'?"

"I found her journal yesterday, lying beside her bed. It was missing and now parts are suddenly showing up in her room."

Rob's face darkened, his eyes narrowing. "Why would you think I had it? Why would I sneak into her room?"

"I don't know. To mess with my mind?" I clung onto Sarah's explanation.

He shook his head. "I can't believe you'd think that." He looked upset and I suddenly felt guilty. But there was something else in his expression...like he was thinking about something and wasn't happy.

"I don't know what to think," I mumbled. "I read this extract... about you..."

The muscles in his jaw tightened. "I don't want to know."

"Well, I want you to know." I grabbed his arm. He looked at me in surprise. "I want you to know how much you hurt my sister."

"I never meant to hurt her," he said. "I really liked Abby; she was so sweet and, of course, beautiful." He glanced at me when he said this and my cheeks involuntarily flushed. "But I didn't love her and I'm not going to apologise for that. D'you want me to apologise for being honest with her? What're you mad at?"

"It sounded like you led her on...you kissed her," I said.

He laughed, shaking his head. "We shared a drunken kiss, one drunken kiss. There was an attraction, nothing deeper."

"But it was deeper for her, she was in love with you," I said.

"And as soon as I realised that I distanced myself," he said.

"And moved onto your next little flirtation?"

"Alright." Anger sparked in his voice. He looked me directly in the eye. "What's this really about?"

I could feel my pulse throbbing in my neck. "What d'you mean? I wanted you to know, to understand..."

"To understand what?" he asked.

"To understand..." I grasped for words; what was I trying to say? "That it's not okay to make a girl feel like she's special, give her your full undivided attention and then just walk away, like they were nothing."

"Okay, so I'm an arse," he said. "I think we covered that at some point the other night."

I sighed in frustration.

"I find people fascinating and like to spend time with them, particularly females...you're so complicated and fragile," he said. "And I forget that sometimes girls read into things a bit too much."

"So it's their fault, for having over-active imaginations?" I said sharply.

"No, it's their fault for not recognising what love really is," he said. "Your sister didn't really love me. She was in lust with me, had a crush, whatever. People throw the term around too loosely. We didn't even have that deep a connection, trust me. When you feel a connection it's something pretty obvious and unmistakable, for both people involved."

"For Abby it was real. I know how she must have been feeling..." I caught my breath, tears burning the back of my throat as I remembered the pain I felt reading her words. I was *not* going to cry again in front of him.

"And I'm sorry about that, but I didn't intentionally upset her," he said. "It's something that has played on my mind a lot. I've thought about how I've acted the past few months with a lot of the girls hanging around and I guess I've been an insensitive idiot."

I folded my arms, feeling stung by his words. He was admitting he was insensitive, an arse, saying *girls read too much into things...* So I must also be just another fascination, getting totally sucked in like the rest of them.

We stopped outside the park, a distant owl hooting from the trees.

"How long are you grounded for?" he asked.

I shrugged. "I don't know."

"You want to sit for a while in the park?"

His face was illuminated under the street lights, his cheek bones so chiselled – how was it even possible to have such a perfect, sculptured face? A longing vibrated through me. I wanted nothing more than to sit with him, to talk to him all night long...but I was still angry with him, I felt I owed it to Abby to just walk away.

"Or we could go to the cemetery again. This time actually visit Abby's grave so I can apologise to her?" His eyes were questioning, like he was asking for my permission.

"She won't be able to hear you," I said.

"Maybe she can," he said. "Don't you sometimes think she's watching you? That you can feel her presence or something?"

I touched the charm bracelet around my wrist and thought back to the weeks after her death when I'd wake up and have an overwhelming sensation that she'd been lying beside me, could almost feel someone gently blowing against my cheek, like she was trying to caress me but only had empty air to offer. I'd been experiencing those sensations less and less lately, but still... something inside me still felt strongly connected to her, almost like part of her occupied my soul.

"Go if you want to. I should get home now."

Rob held out his hand to me. "I want to go there with you. It'll mean more if you can hear my apology to her."

My hand slid into his even although my head told it not to. He held it tight; his thumb gently caressing the back of my hand. A little thrill did a loop around my body but doubts were also curling around to meet it in the opposite direction.

"I don't think it's a good idea for me to keep spending time with you," I said.

The moonlight cast shadows across his face as he looked at me. "I get why you might be wary. But with you, I don't know, you're different. With you I feel a connection."

A sensation like my heart exploding took the breath from me.

"I was confused at the Barn. I didn't want to repeat things all over again, leading you on...but sometimes I think it might be you that's leading *me* on."

I found my voice at this. "What d'you mean?"

"Sometimes I think you like me, then other times, like tonight, it's like you hate me." He paused, looking a bit uncomfortable... almost embarrassed. Not an emotion I thought I'd ever see the calm, composed Rob display.

"Do you...like Michael?"

The question threw me. I laughed at the absurdness of it. "Why on earth would you say that?"

He frowned. "No reason. I just wondered."

"Why would you say that though? Did he say something?"

"It doesn't matter. I think he just likes to wind me up sometimes." Rob shook his head. His expression hardened. "Maybe you should stop hanging around the Barn for a bit."

I dropped my hand from his. "Why? Because you don't want me anywhere near Michael? You're starting to sound a bit like a possessive boyfriend...and you're not even my boyfriend."

He sighed. "It's not that. Michael's just a bit of a bad influence sometimes."

"On who? You? He won't influence me, if that's what you're worried about."

Rob's eyes narrowed. "No, I don't think he could influence you much. I like that about you..."

I hesitated, wondering how much I could probe into Rob's past without upsetting him. "Michael said his parents took you in when you lost yours," I said. "The two of you must be pretty close."

"I guess he's like a brother to me," Rob said.

"Are you an only child?" I asked.

"Yeah." He nodded.

"It must have been hard, losing both your parents," I said.

"Yup," he said. "You don't need me to tell you what it feels like losing someone you love. I also lost my home. My whole life changed overnight."

Rob went on to describe how it felt, adjusting to life with Michael's family, the rivalry that sometimes existed between the two of them, the way in which he never fully felt like he fitted in anywhere. I suddenly felt lucky to still have part of my family; to still have some sense of normality, no matter how messed up things felt at home.

Gently I slid my hand back inside his and squeezed. He closed his eyes and squeezed back.

"I'll come with you, to Abby's grave," I whispered.

We walked there in silence, allowing my mind time to process what he'd said about us. With me he felt a connection...what did that mean; that he wanted to be my boyfriend? I couldn't really imagine him being my boyfriend, doing mundane things like going to the cinema and eating popcorn, but I wanted to know more about him, really get to know him. His hand wrapped around mine felt so right.

The cemetery was officially shut for the night so we squeezed through the gap in the fence, treading carefully in the dark. Rob held my hand tightly as we walked down the path, our trainers scuffing against the gravel. I looked up at the sky, one by one stars popping into view as my eyes adjusted in the darkness, free from the glare of the streetlights. A strange sensation washed over me as I imagined that each of the brightest stars was one of the suicide victims, looking down on us as we walked past their graves.

We walked down the winding path towards the oak tree and I slowed slightly.

"You okay?" Rob asked.

I nodded as we turned the corner and Abby's gravestone came into view. Her name was etched in stone, below which was written: *Beloved daughter, beloved twin. Forever in our hearts.* I knelt down and Rob laid a hand on my shoulder.

"I'm sorry, Abby," Rob whispered. "I never meant to hurt you and wish I'd treated you differently."

"I'm sorry too, Abby, for not being there," I said. I traced a finger around the word twin and regret tugged deep inside. When had we lost that closeness? Had I created the distance?

Something rustled in the distance and I turned my head. Rob stepped back slightly, straining to see.

A figure walked towards us, dressed in white, skirts blowing in the wind.

"Abby?" I whispered, my head spinning.

CHAPTER 18

"Kat? Kat..."

Rob's voice sounded echoey, like he was shouting down a tunnel. He stood over me, his face blurred. The girl dressed in white hung back slightly. Her features formed into a recognisable face. *Not Abby.*

My head dropped back onto the grass, my limbs sinking into the soil.

"Are you okay?" Rob crouched down, wrapping an arm behind my back and pulling me up towards him.

"Take me away," I whispered.

"What?" he murmured in my ear.

I wanted him to carry me off into the night, away from there, away from the grief.

Chloe stepped forward. "Is she okay?"

I regained the use of my limbs and broke away from Rob, standing to face her. "What're you doing here?"

She looked at Rob, then back to me. Her expression was cold, almost angry. "I just felt like talking to Abby."

"You shouldn't hang around here late at night," I said. What I really wanted to say was stay the hell away from my sister, which even in my head sounded completely irrational.

"I'm sorry for...scaring you," she said.

"It's okay, Chloe. Maybe you should go home, we can walk you?" Rob offered.

"No, it's fine. I just live round the corner." She shook her head. She brushed past Rob and I scrutinised her retreating back. She looked nothing like Abby. Was I losing my mind?

"You sure you're okay?" Rob turned back to me.

"Fine," I said dismissively, embarrassed by my meltdown.

"What?" I said as he started to chuckle.

"I don't think a girl has ever fainted in my presence before."

"You just have that effect on me," I said dryly.

"Next time give me some warning so I can catch you."

"You seem very keen to catch me tonight," I said. "But you should know...I can never be caught."

"So I'll just keep trying." He stepped closer.

"I should go home," I said, unnerved by the way he was looking at me.

"You're always trying to run off." He reached for my hand, tracing a finger slowly across my palm, sending little shivers running up and down my spine. He lowered his head towards mine and I could feel his breath on my face, his scent surrounding me, making my mouth water.

My heart thumped against my chest: *boom, boom. Boom boom.*

He gazed into my eyes, like he was searching, wanting to know me. My body arched towards him instinctively. Slowly, his lips touched mine and he gently stroked my hair. His lips were soft and warm; he tasted sweet, like whisky and spearmint. My head spun as our kiss deepened. I pressed my body against his; he pulled me closer, running his hands up and down my back. An explosion of emotion overwhelmed me; passion, excitement, fear...

I pulled back, my hands trembling.

He pulled his jacket around me, holding me close against him. I leaned my head against his chest, listening to the tripping of his heart. Gradually the beat slowed so that it was a dull thump against my ear.

His lips brushed my cheekbone and he whispered in my ear, *"She walks in beauty like the night, of cloudless climes and starry skies, and all that's best of dark and bright, meets in her aspect and her eyes..."*

"I bet you say that to all the girls."

"Only the ones I think will recognise the poet," he said.

"Byron...*She Walks in Beauty,*" I said.

"And you even know the title." He smiled approvingly. "No passing off any of his work as my own then."

"Is that what you usually do?" I teased.

"My cheesy quotations are for your ears only." His expression turned serious as he said, "There's so much darkness everywhere lately. You have a lot of darkness inside of you, but at the same time this amazing light that I don't think you're even aware of...it's an intoxicating mix."

He moved in for another kiss, this one slow and exploratory. My toes tingled.

I broke away reluctantly. "I *really* should get home."

"We could camp out here, sleep under the stars," he said.

"Sure, when it's already heading into the minus numbers," I said.

"You could come back to mine?" His fingers trailed along my lower back and I shivered.

I pulled away. "If my parents get up in the morning and discover I'm not there they will freak."

"Is that the only reason you won't come back?" he asked, eyes teasing.

"I don't think I can trust you," I said.

"You can't." He kissed my neck and I wanted to let him carry me away into the night.

I glanced over at Abby's gravestone and a sensation of guilt consumed me. It felt like I was betraying her and totally disrespecting her memory, standing at her graveside kissing the boy she had been in love with, especially when he had broken her heart.

"You okay?" he said, following my gaze.

"Fine." I nodded, starting to walk back up the path. "Let's go."

The lights were off when we arrived back at my house. I eyed the tree nervously.

"I can't climb up that," I said.

"Well, you can't ring the doorbell," Rob said.

I reached into my pocket and dangled a key. "Back door key. I should be able to sneak in okay…they're both deep sleepers."

"Can I walk you to your back door?"

"No," I said, standing on my tip toes and kissing him on the cheek. "Night."

"Hey." He grabbed my arm and pulled me in for a proper kiss. "Sweet dreams, Kat."

I smiled and walked away.

"When can I see you again?" he called after me.

"I don't know, I'm grounded, remember."

"I'll come by your work," he said.

"Okay." I waved then walked round the back of the house.

I held my breath all the way through the house, crept up the stairs and was relieved to hear gentle snores coming from the direction of Mum and Dad's room.

Once in the safety of my bedroom I climbed into bed, pulling the covers up over my head. His kiss still tingled on my lips. I closed my eyes and replayed the scene over and over, his face imprinted on my brain, his smell still tangled in my hair.

I fell asleep with a smile on my lips, feeling like a light had turned back on inside of me, surrounding me with a glow of happiness.

"What's wrong with you today?"

"Nothing." I smiled as Callum stacked plates on the counter.

He was losing his patience with me as I kept getting orders wrong but I had more important things on my mind than cheese sandwiches and salads.

"Tough morning at uni?" I asked.

"No." He frowned. "I had a very fascinating seminar actually.

It's since coming in here that my day has started to get tough."

"Sorry," I said. "I'm not really focused today."

"So I noticed," he said. "You also have a stupid smile on your face. Have you won the lottery or something?"

"No." I twirled a strand of hair around my finger.

He rolled his eyes and shoved another stack of dishes on the counter. "Start loading the dishwasher, will you, before the afternoon tea crowd comes in."

"Yes, sir," I muttered under my breath. I glanced at the clock. Three. I wondered if Rob would drop by during the afternoon. He hadn't appeared at all the previous day, but then he might have thought I wouldn't be at work on a Sunday.

"What d'you get up to at the weekend?" Callum asked.

"Not much." I shrugged, trying not to grin like a lunatic as I thought about Rob, about the kiss…

"Still grounded?" he asked.

"Hmm." I nodded.

He walked behind the counter and helped me load the dishwasher.

"You get up to anything interesting?" I asked.

"I went to the Barn for a bit on Saturday night," he said.

I looked up in surprise. "I thought you hated the place."

"I do. But Tom is no longer grounded and I knew he'd head straight there so I wanted to keep an eye on him," Callum said.

"Oh." I wondered if he'd talked to Rob.

"I saw your friends Sarah and Jill," he said.

"I don't think Sarah thought much of the place," I said.

"She did look a bit uneasy or something," he said. "Jill seemed to be having a good time though."

"Jill could probably have a good time just about anywhere." I smiled. "I bet Tom was thrilled to have his big brother hanging around."

"He managed to ditch me for some of the night. He kept talking to that Michael guy. I don't like him." Callum frowned.

"I thought it was Rob you didn't like," I said.

"I don't like him either."

"I saw Tom a few days ago in the park."

"Oh, yeah? He never said."

"He seems pretty smart your bro," I said. "I wouldn't worry about him."

"I don't know. I just feel he's not the same lately, like he's really withdrawn or something," Callum said. "This is going to sound crazy..."

"What?" I placed some more cups in the dishwasher.

"I have this theory...he's always in a bad mood after he's listened to that EP."

"What EP?"

"The Relapse one. He'll listen to it over and over on his stereo sometimes at night when he's studying. Then the next morning he'll snap my head off and mope around."

I shot Callum a withering look. "He's sixteen. You expect him to be all sunshine and light and blowing you kisses on his way out the door?"

"Very funny." He paused. "Thing is...I borrowed the CD, and after listening to it for a few hours I started getting these dark thoughts in my head...like really depressive thoughts. It's weird."

The hairs on my arm stood up as I thought back to the nights I listened to the EP. It was dark music, so of course that could affect your mood. I thought back to the night they played at the Barn... the heavy feeling I had the next day when I got up.

"Were they playing the other night at the Barn?" I asked.

"No, not that I heard. Although at one point it looked like Michael was setting up the stage but then Rob left."

Left to come and meet me. A little voice sang inside.

"You've got that strange smile on your face again." Callum shot me a suspicious look.

"Am I not allowed to be happy? Jeeze. You complain that Tom is moping, you complain that I'm smiling."

"I'm not complaining," he said. "I just don't like seeing such a change in my little brother and he won't talk to me about anything."

I thought back to the conversation I'd had with Tom in the park. "Maybe he's in love. That might explain his moping."

Callum looked bemused, then thoughtful. "I've never heard him mention any girls before."

"You just said he doesn't talk to you about anything. He mentioned Chloe's name in our conversation. I bet he's in love with her," I said.

"And she doesn't know he exists?" Callum filled in the blanks.

"I think she's preoccupied by someone a little older."

"That Rob guy?" Callum almost spat.

Just at that moment the door swung open and I don't know which one of us was more surprised to see Rob strolling in. I laughed and Callum shook his head.

"Always turning up, like a bad smell," he muttered under his breath.

I walked out into the cafe, suddenly feeling nervous and awkward. I smiled at Rob but he didn't smile back. The nerves heightened.

"What's up?" I frowned.

Rob stuffed his hands in his pockets. "I'm heading up North for a bit."

"Oh." I searched his eyes for traces of emotion. I couldn't find any. "Why?"

"Me and Michael had a fight. I need to get away from him for a bit, from everything. I've got a friend up North with some studio space and I need to do some research into something."

"What did you fight about?" I asked.

"Just stuff." He sighed. His face softened as he took my hand and looked into my eyes. "I don't really want to leave you just now but

I need to get away."

I felt like I could drown in those eyes. "How long will you be gone?"

"Just a few days. Maybe a week."

An eternity. "We never exchanged mobile numbers."

"I don't have a mobile," he said.

"And you don't have a Facebook page either."

"You been trying to stalk me?" His lips twitched.

"Maybe." I smiled. "But seriously, why don't you have a mobile?"

"I like being unattainable," he said.

I rolled my eyes.

"You got a pen?" he asked.

I reached over the counter and grabbed a pen and paper. He took them from me and began scribbling.

"This is my friend's number." He folded up the bit of paper and slid it under my belt slowly, his fingers lingering against the bare skin of my stomach, sending shudders running through my body down to my toes.

He glanced over my shoulder and I knew Callum must be watching. Rob pulled my head in slowly towards his and kissed me softly on the lips.

"I'll be thinking about you," he whispered.

I tried to say something in response but my mouth just opened and closed, with no words forming.

"And please stay away from the Barn." A darkness fell across his face. "It's important that you stay away from Michael especially."

I frowned. "Is this about you thinking I like him?"

"No." Rob shook his head. "I can't explain it, until I find out more. But please, just try to keep out of his way."

He kissed me on the forehead and before I had the chance to ask him for more explanation, he was already halfway up the stairs. Part of me wanted to run after him but I knew I had to let him go.

I pulled out the piece of paper from underneath my belt and my eyes were drawn to the words he had scrawled under his contact details:

Never has a kiss tasted so sweet. R x

Callum cleared his throat loudly.

"Don't say a word," I said, not turning around to see his disapproving look. I folded the paper carefully into a square and put it in my pocket; capturing his words, keeping them close. I had the feeling this was going to be the longest week of my life.

CHAPTER 19

The next day, Mum and Dad decided I was no longer grounded, as if they had a sixth sense and knew Rob was away so didn't need to worry about my whereabouts. I still intended to go to the Barn, even with Rob's warning. Just because he was fighting with Michael didn't mean I had to stay away; I was determined to see that film.

"D'you want me to come with you?" Sarah offered quietly as she watched me scrape through my rail of clothes.

"It's up to you, d'you want to come?" I glanced at her through the mirror as I held up a black dress.

"Michael seemed a bit...intense...when I saw him at the weekend. He has this weird crazy look in his eyes," she said.

I smiled, yanking my work t-shirt off and pulling the dress over my head in its place. "He's okay, just a bit eccentric or something."

"What d'you reckon him and Rob were fighting about?"

"I don't know. I noticed some tension between them lately but Rob hasn't told me anything specific."

"I reckon they're fighting about you," Sarah said.

I turned to look at her, puzzled. "What d'you mean?"

"I bet Michael doesn't like him getting close to you," she said.

"Why would that bother him?" I held my hair up, wondering if it made me look older if I pinned it.

"Maybe Michael's afraid it'll mess up what they have going at the Barn. I reckon a lot of the young people are drawn there because of Rob and if he becomes unavailable then maybe the allure will be lost."

I let my hair drop back down. "I think you're spending too much time on your Psychology Higher. You sound a lot like Callum actually."

She laughed suddenly and a blush spread across her cheeks. "Don't be stupid. Why would I sound like him?"

"He just likes to psychoanalyse the place." I shot her a curious look. "You look sort of pleased that I compared you to him."

"I don't know what you're talking about." She averted her eyes and picked up a magazine lying on my bed, burying her face in it.

"You know he's not interested in Jill," I said.

"No, but he's interested in you," she mumbled.

"He doesn't really know me though."

"Not like how Rob knows you," she said, a smirk playing on her lips.

I hadn't told her about the kiss but somehow it felt like she already knew. "Rob doesn't really know me either." I turned back to the mirror and stared into my eyes as I lined them carefully. A flash of Abby stared back out at me. Sweet, naïve Abby. Was I also being naïve? I'd convinced myself I wasn't telling Sarah about the kiss because it was a private thing between me and Rob, but part of me suspected it had a lot to do with not wanting her judgement and hearing her reasons for why this was a bad idea.

"So where does your Mum think you're going tonight?"

"Your place." I smiled. "If you come with me you can tell your parents that you're staying for a bit at mine."

"And what if they happen to call each other?"

"They won't. That's the beauty of the modern age." I waved my mobile and shoved it in my bag.

"Unless you switch it off and your parents call my house. Like last time," she reminded me.

"Oh, yeah."

"I'll come if you really want, but the place made me feel like a loser."

I laughed. "What're you talking about?"

"Everyone looked so cool and beautiful. I felt like a geek." She shuddered. "And this creepy old man in a top hat tried to dance with me. Why would they even let an old guy in there?"

"I think he plays the piano sometimes," I said. "And you fit in fine. I think everyone looks so cool because they have their own style so anything goes. No one really gives a shit."

"They're all so beautiful they don't *need* to give a shit," Sarah sighed.

I smiled. "You're awfully philosophical tonight, Miss R." I clicked off my stereo. "Okay. I'm ready to go."

"I'll walk you there if you like." Sarah grabbed her school bag and the two of us headed downstairs.

"Mum, that's us off to Sarah's," I called.

"Okay, don't be too late," Mum called from the living room.

"I won't."

"You'd better not be, young lady," Sarah mumbled in my ear as we headed out the door.

As we turned the corner towards the park I was aware of a car slowing down behind us. I turned to see Callum rolling down his window.

"Hey, you need a lift anywhere?" he called.

"Where you going?" I asked.

"The city library. Got an essay due in the end of the week," he said.

I glanced at Sarah. "That's such a coincidence. Sarah was just saying how she needed to find a book for an essay she's writing."

Sarah's head shot up and she gave me death eyes.

"Well, I can take you now?" Callum offered.

"That's so nice of you." I pushed Sarah towards the car and she swiped at my hands.

"What're you doing?" she hissed.

"Being a good friend."

"Are you coming too?" Callum asked.

"No." I shook my head. "I have to be somewhere."

Sarah hadn't moved.

"Okay," he said. "You coming, Sarah?"

"Sure." She nodded, as if hearing him ask was all she needed to give her the courage to move forward.

I watched as she climbed into the passenger seat, cheeks burning a deep shade of pink. I waved and she flashed me a look that said, 'I cannot believe you have done this'.

"See you," Callum said.

"Bye, have fun." I waved. I mouthed a 'call me' to Sarah before they sped off. Once they got talking she would be fine. Callum would really like her, I was sure of it.

I cut through the park and took my time wandering along the path, letting my mind drift to thoughts of Rob. He hadn't said how far North he was going but I could visualise him in a cottage somewhere, in the countryside, sculpting something in a studio, with a path that led down to a little beach; maybe there would be a cliffside where he could watch the crashing waves below. I could picture us in a cottage, by a beach, listening to the sound of the waves crashing against the shore as we lay side by side…

"Hi, Kat."

I jumped; the voice jarring me out of my daydream.

"Oh, hi, Tom."

"What's happening?" he said.

"Not much. Where you off to?" He was dressed in black jeans and a worn white t-shirt with a faded black and white image on it. His blonde hair was messy, like he'd just washed it and not bothered to comb it.

"I'm off to the Barn. Michael's doing some filming before the poetry night and he asked me to be in a few shots."

"I thought you didn't like being in front of the camera," I said.

"Changed my mind." He shrugged. "Where you off to?"

"The Barn."

"For the poetry night?"

"I didn't know they were having one." My heart sank at the

thought of Michael using this as an excuse to avoid talking to me, especially if he was also filming.

"Don't you go the shortcut?" he asked.

"No."

The question of why neither of us took the shortcut hung in the air unasked. Then I remembered it was in the woods, by the loch, that he got attacked.

"What's your film about?" I asked.

"I'm not really sure. Michael just wants me to talk about what's happening in my life just now, school and stuff."

"And you're happy to talk about that on film?"

"I might make up some stuff." He smiled and I smiled back.

"Hey, you know your brother is a bit worried about you just now," I said.

"Oh, man." Tom shook his head. "Why's he talking about me? I wish he'd just leave me alone, let me breathe."

"He was just worried you seemed a bit...unhappy." I tried to choose my words carefully.

He didn't say anything.

"If you ever need to talk about anything, I'm all ears."

"So you can report back to my big brother?" he said scathingly.

"No," I said. "I wouldn't do that."

"Then why care?"

"Because sometimes I think if I'd said that to my sister she'd still be here today."

We walked on in silence for a bit.

Then Tom said, "I'm not really unhappy you know. So you can tell Callum not to worry. I just miss my old friends sometimes."

"Me too," I said.

He shot me a curious look. "Haven't you lived here all your life?"

"I have," I said. "But when someone close to you dies it's amazing how some people you've known all your life stop knowing how to talk to you."

"That must suck," he said.

"Sometimes." I shrugged. "My best friends are coming around though, so that's all that matters."

"Some of the guys in school think I'm gay."

I looked at him in surprise. "And are you?"

"No," he scoffed.

"So why'd they say that?"

"I don't know. Because they think I look like a girl or something, because my hair's long and I sometimes wear eyeliner and stuff. I refuse to change how I look just because they give me shit."

"Good for you. They're just jealous because you're really good looking."

He looked bashful. "You think I'm good looking?"

"You will break a million hearts one day, you'll see," I said. "Was that why those guys attacked you?"

"Yeah, I guess," he said. "They don't bother me so much anymore. I think they got bored with me."

"I'm glad. Can I tell your brother that part; that you're not getting bother anymore at school?"

"Fine." He sighed. "But don't tell him about the gay taunts. He'll probably start thinking I am, the way I dress sometimes."

I smiled. We turned the corner and walked up the path to the Barn. I knocked on the door and it opened a slit.

"Name?" came a voice from inside.

"Kat and Tom. From Eddison High." I figured this was the easiest way to identify myself.

"I know who you are." The door opened fully and the girl with red hair who had been there the last time looked me up and down. "Rob isn't here."

"I know," I said, feeling slightly unnerved by her penetrating gaze.

"Come in." She held the door open and we stepped inside.

Tom walked up the stairs and I started to follow but she grabbed my arm.

"I used to go out with Rob a while back," she said.

I pulled my arm back, releasing myself from her grip. "So?"

"So, you should know that he'll break your heart," she said.

"I've heard it all before."

"And yet you still fall by his side." Her lips curled into a pitying smile. "Not everyone has been strong enough to survive it."

"Are you talking about my sister?"

"Maybe," she said. "Sophie was left broken. So was Becca. I thought Abby would have known better."

"What about you? Are you one of the strong ones?"

"I'm here, amn't I?" She raised an eyebrow. "I never fell in love; I just enjoyed the attention. It's when you want more, that's when it starts to hurt."

I wanted to tell her that Rob had said with me it was different. With us it *was* more. But I knew how lame that would sound to her...to anyone... A niggling that he had chosen now to disappear up North, just after we had kissed, started to pull at me.

"Enjoy your night," she said.

I turned and walked up the stairs, my back burning with the sensation of her gaze following my every step.

Upstairs, classical music was playing from a turntable. Two boys lay on the floor, both in cut-off jeans and sunglasses, blowing bubbles in the air. One of them laughed every time he stuck his foot in the air to burst them.

"Gasoline rainbows," shouted the other one. "What book's that from?"

Catcher in the Rye, I thought to myself.

"I freakin' love those words. Gasoline rainbows...that's what these are...they're like poetry, man. Stop ruining my poetry." He kicked at the boy's foot and elicited another laugh.

"Don't use all those bubbles. I'm shooting you two next."

I turned my head and saw Michael standing by a camera and tripod, Chloe sitting up on a stool in front of the lens. Her hair was up and she had on heavy make-up; black eyeliner and red lipstick. She was holding a cigarette and had on a white vest and frayed blue jeans and bare feet. She looked beautiful but vulnerable; like a little girl playing dress-up in her Mum's clothes.

Tom was sitting on the sofa out of shot, staring at Chloe, clearly mesmerised by this image of beauty. I now understood why he'd changed his mind about being in Michael's film.

I walked quietly over to a chair across from Tom and sat down, curious to hear what Chloe was saying.

"What are you sad about, Chloe?" Michael prompted.

Chloe took a slow drag of her cigarette and turned to look at the camera. "I thought Rob loved me."

"Did he tell you that he loved you?"

She seemed to ponder this for a moment. "No…but the way he kissed me. It was like he loved me, really soulful, you know?"

"When did he kiss you?"

"A few months ago. We were both sad Abby was gone." She paused and looked down at her hands.

I held my breath. I wasn't sure I wanted to hear her talking about Abby…or Rob.

"I always wished he would look at me the way he looked at her."

"And how did that feel, being in love with someone who wanted someone else?"

"Horrible." Her cigarette shook in her hand, the ash melting onto the floor. "But he wasn't in love with her. I always thought she was so lucky but then he stopped talking to her. And then I hoped he might notice me. And he did…and we had such a good time together. He taught me how to play his guitar. I wasn't any good, but it was fun." She laughed. "And he got me to sing with him one night."

"I remember that. You were pretty good." Michael took his eye off the lens, looking at her directly for a moment.

She smiled at him, almost shyly, which didn't look like Chloe at all.

"So did you just kiss that one time?"

Chloe looked past the camera, her gaze falling directly on me. I held it, waiting to hear her answer.

"No," she said. "We kissed a lot. He's a really good kisser."

A heat was prickling up my arm. I knew Chloe liked Rob but I'd always presumed she'd never actually got anywhere with him. He acted like he didn't even notice her. I felt sick at the thought of them kissing.

"There was one night…when we went down to the cemetery." She turned to look directly at the camera again.

"Why did you go there?" Michael asked.

"To visit the graves of the people we knew, friends, to feel close to them. We did that sometimes," she said. "That particular night I got quite upset."

"It must be hard for you, losing so many friends in such a short space of time," Michael said.

"It's horrible." She shook her head, her eyes filling with tears. "I miss Abby every single day."

Stop talking. A fire was raging inside me.

"So did he comfort you, when you got upset?"

Chloe nodded. "He held me in his arms, told me everything was going to be okay. He made me feel so safe, so *wanted.* And I really believed that everything was going to be okay. And then…"

"And then what?" Michael prompted, leaning in closer to the camera.

Chloe glanced over at me, her lips curling into a slow smile. "And then we slept with each other, under the stars…and it was magical; I couldn't have imagined my first time being any more special than that."

A buzzing sound was building up inside my head. I glanced over at Tom, saw his pained expression; watched Michael's head pop up in surprise, like he needed to look at Chloe properly to believe her words. And Chloe sat there, looking at me, a triumphant smile on her face, telling me she had won. I had lost. *Poor stupid, naïve Kat.*

CHAPTER 20

"You're a liar." I jumped towards Chloe, knocking over my chair.

Michael turned round in surprise. "Kitty Kat." He directed the camera at me.

"Get that camera out of my face." I glared at him.

"Whoa." He held his hands up and turned it back round to face Chloe.

"Switch it off," I said.

"Why?"

"I don't want this on film."

"But it'll make such a great scene," Michael protested.

"Fine." I pulled Chloe's arm and yanked her off the stool.

"Hey," she yelped.

Tom leapt forward. "Kat, don't hurt her..."

I pulled her along the floor, marching her across the room away from Michael's camera lens.

"Let go of me you crazy weirdo," she seethed, struggling against my grasp.

I let go when we were in the far corner, by the piano.

She glared at me, rubbing at her arms. "Can't handle the truth, Kat?"

"Rob wouldn't sleep with you," I said.

She shot me a condescending smile. "Because he's some pious virgin?"

Her words made my brain jolt. Of course he wasn't a virgin. With all these girls throwing themselves at him I *knew* he wasn't a virgin...but...but what? Had I thought he would need to love them to sleep with them?

"You've got it bad." She shook her head. "I told you ages ago.

He has his flavour of the month and then he gets bored."

"Did he sleep with Abby?"

Chloe shrugged. "Probably. She never told me."

"Wouldn't she tell you something like that?" I pressed.

"Abby never spoke about him much at all. It was like she was lost in some secret world," she said. "Like the less she spoke about him, the more she got to keep him, just to herself. Can I go now?"

I stepped back and watched her saunter towards Michael who was standing with an amused expression on his face, like he was loving this; loving the drama and my anguish.

I noticed a phone hanging on the wall and rushed over to it, keying in the numbers I'd memorised.

The phone rang three times before someone answered.

"Hello?" The voice on the other end was female.

I paused. I'd been expecting a male. "Oh, hi...I was wondering if I could speak to Rob?"

"He's not here right now. He's away getting us dinner."

"Are you...his friend...that he's staying with?"

"Yes, I'm his friend, Jess, and this is my place." She laughed. "Who's this?"

Her voice sounded confident, mature. *Her* place. She had her own place and Rob was staying there. Why didn't he tell me he was staying with a girl...*woman*? "It's...Kat." Would he even have mentioned me?

"You want me to leave him a message?"

"No." I hung up, my hands shaking.

"What's up Kitty Kat?"

Michael leaned lazily against the wall.

"Nothing," I snapped.

"You seem a little upset. Would you like a drink?"

"No..." I pondered this, suddenly feeling the need to escape my mind, to numb this feeling of dread that was pressing down on me, making it hard for me to breathe. "What've you got?"

"Come this way." Michael touched my elbow and led me over to a table set up beside the piano. "We have beer, more beer... wine...Jack Daniels...vodka...rum..."

"Wine is fine."

"Wine is fine, you made a rhyme," he laughed. "Quite appropriate really as tonight is poetry night. Are you going to stay for some verse, Kat? It might cheer you up."

He opened a bottle of red and poured me a large glass.

"Maybe," I said.

"You didn't seem too thrilled by Chloe's little revelation. Did you think Rob was saving himself for you?"

"No." I took a large swig of wine. "I just didn't think Chloe was his type."

"He's not fussy, darling." He grinned.

"Has he slept with all the girls who go here?"

"What d'you think?"

"I don't think he has," I said. "I'm still not convinced he did sleep with Chloe. I thought you appeared surprised too, when she said it."

"I think you're being stupid, Kat," he said, picking up a bottle of beer and opening it with his teeth.

I grimaced at his party trick.

"Rob only thinks about Rob. He'll tell you what he knows you want to hear, to get what he wants."

The feeling of dread spread deeper down my body. I refused to believe Rob was lying to me. We had a connection...I could feel it...

Michael took a swig of beer. "He doesn't realise he's tainting your beauty. He's ruining the beauty of it all."

"What d'you mean?"

"You all arrive here, unspoiled, full of life's hopes and dreams and then he steps all over them, fracturing them, fracturing all of you." He shook his head. "That's what life does you know. But when you escape…that's when you get lucky. It gives your life value."

I began to wonder if Michael was under the influence of something heavier than beer.

Tom appeared. He picked up a beer. "That was totally uncool what you did there, Kat."

I looked at him in surprise.

"Chloe didn't deserve that. You didn't even know Rob when she was with him," he said.

My face flushed as I thought about the crazed way I'd grabbed Chloe. "You're right. I was being totally uncool," I said.

He nodded, like he accepted this as an apology. I wanted to tell him that he was too good for Chloe.

"You ready for your shots now, young man?" Michael said. "Everyone else will be arriving soon so we'd better be quick."

"Sure." Tom shrugged.

I followed them back across the room and sat back down on my chair. Chloe was on the sofa, her expression fixed straight ahead. I tried to push images of her and Rob together out of my head. Was this how Abby had felt when Rob moved onto someone else? I squeezed my eyes shut, my head already starting to spin from the wine.

Tom sat up on the stool, looking nervous and uncomfortable.

"Relax," Michael said. This made Tom's shoulders stiffen even more. "Chloe, start talking to Tom, ask him some questions."

Chloe sat up, crossing her legs. "What's your biggest fear?"

Tom glanced at her and blushed. He shrugged. "I don't know."

Michael stepped back from the camera. "Get into the zone, Tom. Forget we're here. Act like you're having a conversation with your alter ego or something."

Tom fiddled with the pendant hanging around his neck, deep in thought as he stared at the ground. "I get scared talking to girls…"

Chloe giggled and Michael shushed her as Tom continued to

talk, still looking at his feet.

Tom went on to talk about a girl he'd liked for a while, confessing his inability to let her know his true feelings. As he described her beauty in poetic detail, the description painted a clear picture of Chloe.

"Man, you should be a writer," Michael said. "Keep going, keep going."

I watched as Chloe's head rose in interest as he talked, how she listened to his words, like they were unravelling her and I championed Tom to go on. How could anyone not become unravelled by his words?

"She always has this kind of coolness about her, a sort of distance from everyone. I think some people read her as being a bit of a bitch but I think she's just scared, like we're all scared...scared that people will realise that we don't have a clue what we're doing. We don't really know how we should be talking, or how we should behave...always thinking about fitting in, but at the same time kind of not wanting to fit in because then we'll just be ordinary and boring. And who likes boring? Boring doesn't get you noticed or chatted up or asked to the dance."

"Look up at the camera," Michael instructed.

Tom lifted his head slowly and pushed a strand of hair out of his eyes.

He really was strikingly good looking. I looked over at Chloe, hoping she could see it too.

"And would you ask this girl to a dance?" Michael said.

"I'd ask her to dance with me every single night of the year. I would never tire of dancing with her, I'm sure."

"And why are you so scared to talk to her?"

"Because she's in love with someone else. Someone a lot cooler than me." He made a face. "And older."

"D'you really think she's in love with him?"

Tom pondered this for a while. "No. I think she's in love with an idea of him."

"What if you're in love with an idea of *her*?"

Tom grinned. "Then it's the best freakin' idea I've ever had!"

A grin spread across Chloe's face, softening her features.

"What would you say to her now, if she was listening?" Michael asked.

"I'd say..." Tom glanced up at the ceiling. "I'd say that she's better than all of this, that I'd like to get to know her, the real her, and that when I heard her sing with Rob that night she broke my heart, her voice was so beautiful."

Chloe clamped a hand over her mouth and squeezed her eyes shut and I realised that she was crying. Tom looked over at her.

"I'd tell her to stop crying because my heart is breaking all over again."

Chloe jumped up and ran across the room. Tom blinked, looking to the camera for answers.

"What did I say?" he said. "I didn't want to upset her..."

"Go after her," I prompted.

Tom's eyes were big and scared.

"Seriously, go after her," I said.

He jumped down off his stool and hurried across the room, running after the girl who was breaking his heart and who appeared to be breaking her own.

Michael shook his head, laughing. "Jesus Christ. Talk about teenage angst."

"You're an ass," I muttered.

"Excuse me?" He swung around on his heel.

"Making them bare their souls, getting them all confused."

"I don't *make* them do anything. They all *want* to talk. He talked a lot of sense, that kid. I like him. Very photogenic too."

"I want to see Abby's film."

"I wondered when you were going to bring that up." He switched off the camera, unhooking it from the tripod.

People started to arrive, footsteps clambering on the stairs, laughter and chat drowning out my words.

"I want to see it, Michael."

He nodded distractedly, turning to greet friends. "You will, Kat. Just not tonight." He zipped his camera into a bag and took another swig of beer.

"Hey, Mike." A guy wearing a long dark coat and hat punched him playfully on the shoulder. "Looking forward to some eloquent words from you this evening."

"I'm going to be reading the words of someone else tonight I think," Michael said. He turned to me. "Are you going to be joining us?"

"Yes." I took another gulp of wine, the alcohol swirling in my brain. If Rob was elsewhere having a nice dinner with some girl, I wasn't going to sit around pining for him.

"Good, there's a poem I'm going to read which I think you'll enjoy," he said.

"Hey, man I thought you were going to film us." One of the boys with the sunglasses was in Michael's face.

"Another time. Why don't you read one of your poems tonight, Dave?"

Dave smiled a dreamy smile. "Cool, yeah, I could read some of my stuff."

"Great." Michael walked over to the multimedia room and I followed. He unlocked the door and started to push it open then stopped when he noticed me behind him. "Kat, I'm going to show you the film, but just not tonight."

"Fine," I said. "I just wanted to see what the room looks like."

He opened the door a slit, the light from outside illuminating some desks but nothing much else. He shoved his camera and tripod down on the floor then shut the door and locked it, placing the key around his neck and tucking it under his shirt.

I stepped aside to let him past.

The phone on the wall started to ring and my heart lurched. It could be Rob.

Michael reached across to answer. "Hello?"

I watched his expression as he spoke.

"She's not available to speak to right now."

"Is it Rob?" I asked, stepping closer, trying to hear the voice on the other end.

"No need to worry about anything, my good friend." Michael hung up and smiled at me. "Wrong number."

"That was him, wasn't it?" I reached for the phone and Michael caught my wrist.

"Leave it, Kat."

I tried to pull away but his grip was too tight. His eyes bore into mine.

"Just relax and enjoy yourself tonight. Just forget about him. He'll be back soon and then you can talk." Michael's voice was soothing, almost convincing. "He doesn't like it when girls act desperate. It makes him run."

I relented and relaxed. Michael dropped my hand and put an arm around my shoulder. "Now come and listen. D'you like poetry?"

I nodded, watching as girls pulled back curtains and lit candles up at the stage area where I'd first watched Rob play in the band. That seemed like such a long time ago, that first night we'd met. The guy in the long black coat was helping the red-haired girl lay out cushions and rugs for people to sit on.

"What poetry d'you like?" Michael asked.

"Old stuff like Emily Dickinson, Shelley, Byron…" I tried to remember who I'd read.

"Keats?"

"I think so."

"Good. I thought I'd read some Keats this evening." He walked over to the table by the piano and I followed. "More wine?"

I looked down at my glass and realised it was empty. "Okay..."

He filled it up to the top.

"Where d'you think Tom and Chloe went?" I asked, looking round the room.

"I think they're in my office." Michael glanced over at the open door. "I didn't see that coming with Tom. I had no idea." He scratched his chin, deep in thought. "Each other's saving grace."

"What d'you mean?" I asked.

"But who's your saving grace?" His gaze fixed on me.

"I don't know what you mean," I mumbled.

"Don't think you can depend on Rob." He leaned in towards me, his lips close against my ear. "He'll never really be there for you. So, who is? Who can you really depend on?"

I wanted to tell him to shut up but something inside of me was breaking, acutely aware that I was standing alone with no one beside me. Sarah had wanted to come with me. *But not really,* a little voice reminded me. My parents were there for me...*but have hardly spoken to you since Abby's death...they're too caught up thinking about her...*

"Why has Rob disappeared so abruptly, Kat? Think about it."

"He's just visiting his friend..."

"What friend? He told me he was going to visit Mum and Dad." A smirk played on Michael's lips.

I felt sick. Why would he say that to Michael? Did that mean Jess was someone more significant and he knew Michael might blab all to me?

"Jess," I said quietly.

Surprise flickered in Michael's eyes, almost shock. Not the reaction I expected.

"You know her?"

A distant look washed over his face, like he was trying to piece things together. "She's an old friend of ours." He glanced back at the phone, as if he was pondering something.

Then in a flash he had resumed an arrogant air. "A very *experienced* friend. And I'm guessing you're not."

"You don't know anything about me."

"Your blush is telling me all I need to know," he chuckled.

"It's from anger."

"Why so angry, Kitty Kat?"

"Stop trying to make me doubt him,"

"I don't think I need to try." He stepped away from me. "Take a seat. The poetry is about to begin."

I tried not to picture Rob with his friend. Tried not to picture him with Chloe, Abby, that redheaded girl… I gulped down more wine. Maybe if I'd gone home with him the other night he'd still be around. *Don't be so pathetic and desperate, Kat.*

People were taking seats near the stage. I sat further back, watching as Michael took centre stage.

"Evening, ladies and gentlemen." He smiled. "I want to start off the evening with an abridged version of a Keats poem, *Ode on a Grecian Urn*. I'll be taking us straight into the second verse…"

He paused and scanned the audience, his gaze resting upon me. I fixed a steely gaze right back at him and he smiled.

My attention wandered as he began to read and I glanced around the audience, recognising a few faces from previous evenings. Then lines started to penetrate my brain:

"…Fair youth, beneath the trees, thou canst not leave
Thy song, nor ever can those trees be bare;
Bold Lover, never, never canst thou kiss,
Though winning near the goal…yet, do not grieve;
She cannot fade, though thou hast not thy bliss
For ever wilt thou love, and she be fair!"

He paused to pick up his beer and took a sip.

"Ah, happy, happy boughs! that cannot shed
Your leaves, nor ever bid the Spring adieu;
And, happy melodist, unwearied,
For ever piping songs for ever new;
More happy love! more happy, happy love!
For ever warm and still to be enjoy'd,
For ever panting, and for ever young;
All breathing human passion far above,
That leaves a heart high-sorrowful and cloy'd,
A burning forehead, and a parching tongue."

A chill ran up my spine as I listened to the final lines;

"Who are those coming to the sacrifice...
...what little town...
...Is emptied of this folk, this pious morn?
And, little town, thy streets for evermore
Will silent be...
...When old age shall this generation waste,
Thou shalt remain, in midst of other woe...
...'Beauty is truth, truth beauty'...that is all
Ye know on earth, and all ye need to know."

An image of Abby flashed into my mind, a memory of her spinning me round one night months ago, smiling as she sang, *"Beauty is truth, truth beauty. That... is all...you need to know."*

CHAPTER 21

Michael bowed before his audience but I didn't join in the applause.

The words of the poem circled my head. It was one I was familiar with; we had studied it in an after-school creative writing class. A class that Abby hadn't been in.

Michael was at the drinks table, downing more beer. I headed over, placing my empty wine glass beside him.

"Can I fill you up?" he asked.

"No."

He turned to watch the next performer.

"Interesting choice of poem," I said.

"It's one of my favourites."

"What d'you like about it?" I probed.

"I like the concept."

"Of what?"

"You seem a smart girl, Kat. What d'you think it's about?"

"I know what it's about. I asked you what you *like* about it."

"People have different interpretations. What d'you think the poem is saying?"

"He's admiring the beauty of the urn...how the figures on it get to stay frozen in time, forever in love, forever young, remaining untainted by life, by time," I said slowly, looking around at the images of the dead stars aligning the Barn walls. "A bit like the icons here."

He smiled. "See, I knew you were a smart girl, Kat."

"Abby quoted parts of the poem to me."

"Did she?"

"Did you read it to her?"

"I've read it a few times before, here, on nights like this," he said. "I think she liked the concept too."

I closed my eyes. *Forever young, forever beautiful on film, in paintings…could she be that lost…to want that…?*

"You're looking a bit tired and pale, Kat. If you want, you can go and take a nap in my office."

"I'm going home." I glanced at my watch. I didn't feel like another grounding after I'd just been freed. "I'll be back tomorrow."

"I'll have the popcorn waiting," he said. "I'm at art school during the day so let's make it an evening screening."

"Okay." I turned to walk away, my mind filled with Abby, Keats, and even more unanswered questions.

"Oh, and Kat…"

I looked back at Michael.

"I'm glad you understood the concept of the poem. It's an important part of my Degree show and it will make everything clearer tomorrow…when you watch the film."

A shiver ran down my spine as his lips slid into a vacant smile. I hurried down the stairs, my phone beeping to alert me that I had two voicemails.

Sarah's and an unrecognised number were listed in my missed calls. I knew the second one would have been Rob, probably demanding to know why I'd gone to the Barn when he'd warned me not to. Let him sweat. If he could do what he pleased, then I could also do whatever I wanted. I switched off my phone, wishing I could switch off my brain with it.

Work passed slowly the next day. Every time the door opened a pathetic longing of hope ran through me; that it would be Rob, arriving home early from his trip to give me a proper explanation. My mobile burned in my pocket, the temptation to dial his friend's number almost taking over. *Desperation is never pretty, Kat.*

As soon as the clock hit six I hurried outside and was surprised to see Callum leaning against a wall, waiting.

"Why's your phone switched off?"

"What're you doing here?" I asked, ignoring his question.

"I wanted to talk to you," he said. "Sarah tried to call you last night."

"I know; I was going to phone her when I got home. What's up?"

"She came across an interesting article in a book we found at the library last night..."

"Seriously," I laughed. "You came here to tell me about some book?"

"Just listen." He sighed impatiently.

"Okay," I said. "Do your talking as we're walking; I need to go home and get changed."

"It was about this invention, called The Mosquito, an alarm which some guy put together to try and counteract anti-social behaviour amongst young people. It emits a really high-pitched sound, like at eighteen hertz or something, that only people below the age of twenty-five can hear."

"Fascinating," I said.

"It got me to thinking; what if there's something running in the background of Relapse's songs, like some high frequency sounds that only young people can hear."

"Are you being serious?"

"Sarah agreed with me, she thought it could be possible..."

I rolled my eyes, on the verge of telling him Sarah agreed because she wanted in his pants. "What kind of sounds are you talking about anyway?"

"I don't know, like subliminal messages, you know like how they used to put subliminal images of drinks and food in the adverts at the cinema to make you think you were hungry or whatever."

"So Relapse put what exactly in their music? Messages telling kids to kill themselves?"

Callum shot me a nervous look, obviously detecting the notes of anger in my voice.

"D'you realise how ridiculous you sound right now, Callum?"

He started to look a bit sheepish. "I know it sounds totally 'out there' but it gave us both chills reading that article, like we were supposed to come across it. The book fell open at the page and everything."

"Like some intervention from God," I said.

"Fine." He folded his arms. "Go ahead and mock me."

"How was your evening at the library anyway?"

"Good. Sarah's really smart; she helped me with my essay... embarrassing to admit really that a high school kid is helping me with my uni work."

I smiled. "She'll be at uni pretty soon, not that far behind you."

"True... I heard you were at the Barn again. Tom said he spoke to you and I want to thank you for whatever you said as he was like a new person today." Callum shook his head. "We managed to have a proper conversation over breakfast and everything. I can't remember the last time we exchanged more than two full sentences."

"I think Chloe's probably the one you should thank."

"Yeah?" He raised an eyebrow. "He didn't mention her."

We reached a crossing in the road.

"Are you heading to the Barn again this evening?" he asked.

"Yeah."

"Just be careful."

I thought back to Rob's warning. "Why does everyone act like it's some dangerous place to go?"

"Tom said something this morning, actually; about it having a dangerous allure."

"Yeah well, I'm not going for social purposes tonight."

He looked at me curiously. "Taking an art lesson or something?"

"Or something," I said, not wanting to tell him about the film.

"See you at work."

He waved and I hurried home. The phone was ringing as I opened the door. I ran to answer.

"Hello?"

Silence.

"Hello?"

"Do you miss her?"

Him.

"Don't you want to join her?"

The voice was muffled, like his hand was covering the mouthpiece. I held my breath, waiting to see if he would continue with no interaction.

A few seconds passed before he spoke again. "Why so quiet?"

An image of this faceless person standing in the phone box beside Eddison Woods flashed into my mind. I reached into my pocket and turned on my mobile.

"Why're you trying to hide your voice?" I asked.

"I have nothing to hide."

"So tell me your name."

Silence. I searched through my mobile for music tracks.

"I bet you miss her a lot. Life must feel pretty empty these days without her. You'd find peace if you joined her."

I clicked play on one of Relapse's songs and held my mobile up to the receiver for a minute, then spoke: "I want you to listen to this."

"Who is it?"

Was the person just pretending not to recognise the music? The voice had no real emotion so was hard to read. I laid the receiver on the table, positioning my mobile beside it then ran out the door.

My feet pounded against the pavement as I ran, excitement powering me on at the thought of catching him unawares, getting to finally discover who this creep was. The track would only last about another four minutes. He would be sure to hang up when there was no response when it ended. I ran past the park, a stitch stabbing at my side. *Faster, faster, come on Kat...*

Which end of Eddison Woods was the phone? I tried to picture seeing a phone box. I really hoped it was the closest end. It would take too long to run through the woods.

I turned the corner and a phone box came into view at the neck of the woods. A final surge of adrenaline shot through me, carrying me through the last steps. As I approached I squinted, trying to see past the graffiti etchings and grime on the glass.

My legs buckled as I slowed to a halt. I fell against the glass door, every inch of my body deflating as I realised there was no one inside. The phone was off the hook, receiver swinging from side to side. I opened the door, grabbing the receiver and holding it against my ear. There was no dial tone, just a crackling on the other end: *An open line*. He'd been here.

"Damn it." I slammed the receiver down. Traces of a scent circled the air. I picked up the receiver again and sniffed. Aftershave, subtle but definitely there. I breathed it in; it was musky...familiar...*Rob. No.* My back slammed against the door as I recoiled in disbelief. *Not Rob. He wouldn't do this.* I started to shiver uncontrollably, a tremor running down my leg. Then I remembered; *He's not here. It can't be him.* And the shivering subsided slightly. *It's just someone who smells like him...* The tremor in my leg continued as his smell surrounded me, taunted me.

I pushed the door open, taking in large gulps of air from outside. My temples were throbbing from the exertion, confusion and the questions, always so many unanswered questions.

"I need your answers, Abby," I whispered, running in the direction of the Barn.

CHAPTER 22

"Name?"

An eye peeked through the gap in the half opened door.

"Kat."

"As in pussy?" The voice sniggered.

"Let me in; I'm here to see Michael."

"He's not here."

I checked my watch. Six forty-five.

"I'll wait."

"You do that." The door shut in my face.

"I meant inside," I shouted.

The door opened and my tormentor chuckled. He was wearing weird bug-eye sunglasses and a bowler hat, with streaked blonde hair peeking out from underneath. He pushed his sunglasses forward, peering at me intently.

"I know you, but you look different..." he said.

I ignored him, walking up the stairs.

He followed close behind. "You used to have blonde hair. Black looks good on you though, gives you a little gothic edge. I've not been here in a bit...when you stopped coming it wasn't so much fun. Why did you stop coming?"

We reached the main room and I turned to him.

"Because I died."

He laughed, pulling off his sunglasses. "Right on. Like you've killed off the blonde in you and now you've resurrected your dark twin?"

"Something like that," I said, nearly laughing along at his obliviousness to how accurate a description that could be.

Music was playing loudly and a girl in a black dress and fringed jacket was dancing on top of a table in the middle of the room. She waved her arms around, her long dark hair swishing from side to side. Her moves were repetitive, hypnotic almost. I watched in awe at how completely unselfconscious she was.

"That's Dani," the boy said, following my gaze. "She's hot. Totally wasted. But hot."

He walked over to the sofas and pulled back a cushion, revealing a row of beers. "Want one?" He held up a bottle, poised to throw.

I shook my head no.

He sat down and rested his feet on the table, peering up at Dani as she danced. "Dance, dance, dance, Dani, dance!"

I walked across the room, heading towards the curtained area where Rob stored art materials.

"You still thinking of going to Art school?" the boy shouted in my direction.

I hesitated. "No."

"You should, you know. Your paintings were freakin' awesome. Michael was just being an idiot."

"My paintings?" I asked, pulling back the curtains, the fumes of paint and turpentine overwhelming.

"You shouldn't have listened to him. When has he ever painted something half decent anyway?"

"I guess he knows what he's talking about though," I said hesitantly, wondering what Michael had said.

"No way. They were awesome and he never should have done that. Is that why you stopped coming?"

I looked at the photos along the walls, black and white arty shots of young people. *That girl*, the one I had started to look at the last time before Rob had distracted me. I pulled it down off the wall. It was Sophie, sitting on a stool, hair up and cigarette in her hand. Like Chloe the other night...

"What d'you mean? What did he do?" I asked absentmindedly, looking back at the other pictures.

"Are you kidding me?" The boy said incredulously. "When he put your paintings on the bonfire. You cried all night; how can you not remember?"

Abby had always looked for reassurance, needed constant praise...a real people pleaser. Michael burning her paintings would have been devastating. Another rejection.

A row of Polaroids was pinned up on the wall. A boy holding his hand up which was in clear focus, the word *Beauty* written in black across his palm; the next one displaying *Is* between his knuckles, the next one with *Truth* written across his other palm. Then the photos changed to shots of his face; *Truth* scrawled down the side of his cheek; *Beauty* written across his forehead. I looked into his eyes. *Martin.*

"Oh hey, Michael. We were just talking about you..." I heard the boy say.

"What're you doing in here?" Michael pulled back the drapes, accusation in his eyes.

"Just looking," I said.

He glanced at the pictures on the wall. "You're early. Come and sit down while I change."

He waited for me to walk out. I did as he said and he pulled the drapes shut.

"Good day?" I asked.

"Fine." He shrugged his jacket off and threw it over beside the boy. "Nice moves, Dani."

Dani kept dancing, even between songs her body gyrated; her arms still swung.

"How can she keep that up?" I asked.

"She's in a trance," the boy said. "Come and sit; have a beer."

I shook my head. "I'm okay."

Michael re-appeared, wearing a loose white t-shirt that was slashed into a V shape to his chest. A key swung on the long chain around his neck.

"Give me a minute to set things up," he said.

"Okay." I nodded, watching him walk over towards the Marilyn Monroe door.

"What's he setting up?" the boy asked.

"He's showing me a film."

"Which one?"

"One that he made."

"Weren't you in one? I remember seeing you sitting in front of the camera, getting filmed."

"Yeah, it's that one."

"Cool. You get to see yourself on screen." He slapped his thigh. "Can I watch?"

"I'd rather just watch it myself first," I said.

"Aw, alright. Let me see it soon, though."

There was a thud as Dani stopped dancing and fell to her knees, nearly sliding off the table.

"Whoa." The boy jumped up and steadied her, his hand grasping her shoulder.

"Is she okay?" I stepped forward, trying to determine if her bowed head was due to tiredness or something more serious.

"Dani." The boy placed a hand under her chin and slowly tilted her face up, smoothing back her hair with his other hand.

There was a dreamy smile on her face as she swayed slightly.

"She's okay." He turned to grin at me. "She's just coming out of it."

Michael re-appeared. "Ready, Kitty Kat?"

I followed him to the Marilyn Monroe room and wondered if he was going to stay and watch it with me.

We stepped inside the room and my eyes were drawn to the candles flickering on a table in front of the TV screen; an open bottle of wine and two full glasses telling me that he did intend to stay.

"Sit." Michael gestured towards the sofa.

I sat down and he flicked off the light, the candles casting shadows against the walls as he walked back over to sit beside me. As my eyes adjusted to the dark they were drawn to a montage of paintings and photos arranged in a mural on the back wall. Images of Abby, Sophie, Martin, Becca...all of the suicide victims were smiling back at me.

"Who put that together?" I asked.

"Me and a couple of others."

"Why?"

"As a tribute to them, like a little shrine of remembrance."

"It's creepy; I don't like it," I said. "They're not the same as your dead film star posters you know."

"No, they're not," he said.

I stood up, walking over to the mural, wanting to get a closer look, but also conscious that I was purposely delaying the moment I would have to watch my sister on screen. The words 'Truth is Beauty' looped around the top of the photo montage. All of them were beautiful, so young, so free looking. I lingered on the photograph of Abby.

"What's with the 'Truth is Beauty' quote being everywhere?" I turned to Michael.

"It's the title of my degree show," he said matter of factly.

I frowned, a horrible sensation dawning. "You're not featuring them in your show, are you?"

He smiled. "You're piecing things together quicker than I thought, Kitty Kat..."

"There is no way Abby is going to feature in your show." I started to pull at the photograph of my sister, the corners stuck fast against the cardboard backing. What was wrong with him? How could he possibly think this was an okay thing to do?

"Kat, please..." Michael appeared at my side, grabbed my wrist. "I thought you wanted to watch the documentary. We've got time to talk after."

I paused, thinking it would be best to see the documentary first in case Michael changed his mind. "Okay." I followed him back to the sofa, sitting on my hands to stop them from shaking. I still wasn't sure I was ready to see Abby on screen.

"That boy out there…he said you threw Abby's paintings on a bonfire," I said as Michael picked up the remote control. "Why did you do that?"

He sighed loudly. "That boy has a big mouth."

"He said she was really upset. You must have known how bad that would make her feel, doing that."

"She wanted to use them for a portfolio of work," he said. "And I told her there was no way that kind of painting would get her into Art School."

"So you *destroyed* them?"

He shrugged. "I was drunk, we needed firewood. And I thought it'd push her to paint better."

"I don't believe that's why you did it," I said.

"So why did I do it?" His lips curled into an amused smile.

"I think you did it to make her feel like crap."

Michael shook his head. "Why would I do that? Only a weak, pathetic man would feel the need to do that."

"Touché," I mumbled.

"Kitty Kat." He tutted. "Not nice."

"I'm not here to be nice."

He smiled. "Always on the defensive. Such a contrast to Abby's trusting nature."

"Did Abby trust you?"

Michael ran a finger along the edge of his glass. "She trusted Rob. And her friends. But Chloe let her down, didn't she…going after the man she loved."

"Were they all in love with Rob?" I glanced over at the mural. "Even the boys?"

Michael smiled. "He's good, but not *that* good."

"So why d'you think they did it?"

"They were all sensitive souls, impressionable and feeling suffocated by this small-minded town," he said. "They were desperate to be more, to escape."

"Abby was always happy..."

"Until?"

I looked at him questioningly.

"You sounded like you wanted to add on an 'until' to that statement," he said.

"Okay, until she came here, met all of you."

"Maybe coming here opened up her eyes to bigger things."

"Bigger things that you made her think she could never have?" I challenged.

"Why don't we watch the film and you can hear her speak," he said.

A shiver ran through me at the thought of hearing Abby speak new words, words that I had never heard, forming a different memory from the ones I was wearing out in my head, replaying them over and over to try to stop her from disappearing completely.

"How can you afford to run this place?" I asked, stalling him.

"Richie Rich Rob."

I frowned. Rob had never given me the impression he was wealthy. Michael registered my confused expression and went on to explain.

"Rob is set for life thanks to his late parents. His Dad was some entrepreneur and his lawyer helped Rob invest his inheritance wisely."

"It must have been weird for you, having Rob come to stay forever," I said.

A look of surprise flickered in Michael's eyes, like no one had ever considered this before, or at least never thought to talk to him about it.

"He had nowhere else to go. No other family lived here, no other family wanted him."

"That was nice of your parents to take him in."

His eyes darkened. "Are we watching this film or not?"

His composure had slipped and I wanted to probe further but I also wanted to see the film. Angering him was probably not the best plan. "Okay, go ahead."

The screen crackled for a few seconds then Abby's face appeared.

CHAPTER 23

"Is it on?" Her voice was quiet and uncertain.

I stared, transfixed with this foreign image of my sister sitting on a chair, her eyes wide and expectant. Her hair was curled and hung loose around her shoulders. She always liked to curl her hair; she tried to do mine for me but it always resisted, unfurling back to poker straight within hours. "Your hair doth protest," she used to say in what she termed her 'important telephone voice'.

She was wearing a white dress I didn't recognise.

"What should I say?"

The voice off camera was muffled and the words were indistinguishable.

Abby nodded then looked directly into the camera. She paused and I imagined that she was actually seeing me, appearing from another dimension to say hello, to tell me that she was doing okay.

"I've been coming here for a while now. Some older girls in school told me about it; they used to talk to me in the toilets, ask me where I bought my shoes and stuff. They told me to only tell select friends as they explained it's like an exclusive place. Only certain types of people get in."

"What kind of people?" I could now clearly hear Michael's voice off camera.

"Well, like no neds or losers," Abby said matter of factly. *"I like how there's no neds here. There's so many gangs around town and I hate it."*

"What d'you think of Eddison?"

"Total loserville," she said, rolling her eyes in a way I'd almost forgotten. I missed her rolling her eyes at me. *"Loads of people have lost their jobs; all the local businesses can't survive. And there's*

nothing to do. One stupid little cinema that only shows three films. Me and my friends used to always get the bus into the City but we spend more time here now."

"What d'you like about the place?"

"Everything. It's so cool." She smiled, then laughed. *"The other night this guy asked to paint my picture and he was so drunk he kept missing the canvas. And there's this cool old guy in the top hat."* She motioned with her hand. *"He is so amazing on the piano. He was playing Bach the other day and it sounded beautiful."*

She looked down at her hands, then off into the distance. *"It's like it's sort of become my whole life, like nothing else matters. No one else matters, just this place, the people here."*

"Anyone in particular?"

She hesitated, looking back at the camera, her eyes wide and expressive. So trusting. *"Rob."*

Her face changed slightly when she said his name, like a light came on behind her eyes.

"What's so great about him?"

She smiled, a really pure happy smile. As she went on to describe how beautiful and popular he made her feel, and so special and alive, I wanted to look away. It could have been me, sitting there, speaking those words. *Have we both been stupid, Abby?*

The scene cut to the main room of the Barn where people were dancing. The camera panned, capturing the crowds. Then Sophie appeared in front of the camera and waved. She motioned for the camera to follow her and Michael did, filming her back as she danced through the crowds. She led him to Abby, who was spinning around, her dress billowing out around her, like an angel in flight.

The camera zoomed in on her laughing face. Then it panned back out to reveal her dance partner: Rob. He pulled her in close, murmuring something in her ear that made her smile coyly. The memory of his words to me whispered in my head: *You're so beautiful.*

"He's a good dancer, eh?" Michael said, his voice bringing me back to the present.

I didn't respond, feeling a horrible surge of jealousy as I watched Rob dance with Abby in that way...like he had danced with me.

The scene cut to Sophie, sitting on a stool.

"There's more of Abby later; want me to fast forward?" Michael asked.

I nodded, desperate for more insights into my sister's head.

We sat in silence as a blur of faces played out in double speed in front of us.

"Stop." I sat forward, seeing Abby re-appear.

Michael rewound a few frames then hit play.

"Who's your best friend?"

Abby hesitated, a flicker of sadness visible in her eyes. *"It used to be my sister."*

My body tensed.

"Your twin?"

Abby nodded. *"Kat."*

"Are you identical?"

"We used to be," she said quietly. She looked at her hands and a smile spread across her face like she was remembering something funny. *"We used to wear the same clothes and did the typical twin thing of pretending to be each other. Kat was always great at mimicking my mannerisms; she even fooled Mum and Dad a lot of the time."*

Abby never knew that I did this at times when she wasn't aware of the trick either. Times when she'd be busy upstairs playing and I was curious to see how Mum acted alone with her, if she treated her any differently. I once helped Mum bake a whole batch of fairy cakes as Abby and I was relieved that she still told me off for licking the spoon as I'd always suspected they were softer on my sweet sister.

"I'm guessing you don't wear the same clothes anymore then?" Michael's voice prompted off screen.

"No." Abby frowned. *"You might not even realise we were twins anymore."*

"You don't look happy about that."

"I am. It would be pathetic looking the same at this age." Abby shook off her frown. *"It's kind of suffocating having someone walking around as your shadow."*

The hairs on my arm prickled as I heard my own words being spoken back at me. I'd said – more like yelled – that to Abby when she'd told me my freshly-dyed black hair made me look like a freak and had demanded to know why I'd done it. She'd cried and I'd rolled my eyes at her tears, telling her not be so dramatic.

"We used to be really close, like we could almost feel each other's emotions and I always knew just by looking at her what she was thinking. We can't do that anymore." She looked wistful. *"Sometimes I wish we could. Kat feels so distant these days."*

You were the one who was distant from *me,* I wanted to say.

"Why d'you think that is?" Michael asked.

Abby shrugged. *"We're not interested in the same things anymore and I find it hard to talk to her."*

"Why's that?"

"I don't know. It just feels like we've become disconnected and I don't really know how to fix it."

I clenched my jaw as tears welled up. My chest tightened at the strain of trying to keep my emotion in check. Michael was watching me intently, and I refused to cry in front of him.

"Want me to pause it?" He sat forward, taking a sip of wine.

"No," I shook my head, relieved that my voice was still steady. "I want to keep watching."

"Have some wine." He handed me a glass.

It burned my throat as I took too big a gulp.

Michael touched my wrist and shot me a strange smile. "Not

too much, Kat. Save some for later."

I shushed him as the screen went fuzzy. "What's happening?"

"The next part is filmed a few months later," Michael explained.

Abby re-appeared on screen and I shivered. She looked different; the light had gone from her eyes and her face looked thinner; she had a hauntingly beautiful quality about her that unsettled me.

She was listening to a voice off screen that we couldn't hear.

"It's been hard," she responded, nodding. *"Everyone's a bit scared and confused."*

"Did you know what they were planning?"

"No," Abby said sharply. *"They didn't tell us anything. I was just talking to Sophie a few days ago..."*

There was a blip then Abby re-appeared.

"She broke down at that point," Michael informed me.

I didn't look at him, thinking he almost seemed gleeful at the drama.

"Why d'you think they did it?"

I watched Abby's face intently, looking for a knowing, for an understanding. *Why did you all do it, Abby?*

"I don't know," she answered sadly. *"It can be hard being seventeen."*

"Why?" Michael asked, off screen.

She started to fiddle with her charm bracelet, spinning the moons and stars around the main band. I automatically touched my wrist, mimicking her movement.

"There's this feeling that every detail of the day is so devastatingly important that if you take one wrong turn it will somehow irrevocably affect the rest of your life."

Michael placed his wine glass on the table, slapping his forehead. "I got the word wrong, she said 'turn' not move, that's right..."

I glared at him, remembering back to his paraphrase.

"Were they unhappy here then?"

Abby shrugged. *"Sometimes it can be hard to see the bigger picture, especially in a town as small as Eddison. I know Sophie planned to escape as soon as she could."*

"So this was her idea of escape?"

"She had big plans, so no." Abby sat on her hands. *"I just don't understand why she would give up on her dreams. She was so smart and pretty."*

"Was she in love with Rob?"

Abby looked up, startled by the question. *"She liked him loads but so do a lot of girls here."*

"He used to spend a lot of time with her but seemed to move his attentions to you. That must have hurt her a lot; seeing one of her friends with the boy she wanted to be with."

"It wasn't like that..." Abby said slowly, looking confused, like she wasn't sure herself how things had played out.

"You're a creep," I said to Michael and he shot me a mock hurt look.

"I'm sure you both did nothing to intentionally upset her. You have fun here, don't you Abby?"

Abby started to fidget with her bracelet again, like she was deep in thought. *"You know, having sensitive and creative people together here in their own little world isn't always good. It sometimes affects your state of mind, like it's easy to lose a grip of reality."*

"What did you think of the Andy Warhol book I gave you to read?"

I glanced over at Michael and he held up his wine in a 'cheers' gesture. He was always changing the subject when topics veered in directions he didn't like.

"It's okay. His life was kind of interesting," she said. *"You've done a good job of creating a space just like the Factory."*

"Thank you. He was quite perceptive don't you think, like how he said everyone was going to be famous for fifteen minutes. That's

what our culture has become really, hasn't it?"

"I guess. I never really thought about that. We've got all that crappy reality TV." Abby made a face. *"So maybe no one stands out anymore. Though they really get noticed when they die."* Her eyes focused on something in the distance, darting to different points on the walls and I knew she must be looking at the posters of dead stars. *"Death freezes that fifteen minutes, like it preserves their fame and they're remembered."*

"Will you remember Sophie and Martin and all the other suicide kids?"

Abby nodded solemnly and looked directly at the camera. *"Always."*

The screen faded to black.

Michael pressed pause on the remote. "That's all the clips of Abby."

I nodded, losing the ability to speak. All I could do was keep nodding. I was helpless against the tears which started to flow; messy loud tears that I couldn't control.

Michael started to move closer.

"Don't touch me." I backed against the arm of the sofa, the hard edge digging into my back.

"Here, dry your eyes." Michael pulled a tissue from his pocket.

I squeezed the tissue against my eyes, trying to stop the tears from flowing. *Stop crying, stop crying...*

"I'm sorry it upset you," he said.

"It's so hard...seeing her like that," I tried to explain.

"I know, but you insisted."

"I wanted answers." I wiped at my cheeks. "But she seemed as confused as the rest of us. She wasn't doing it for fifteen minutes of bloody fame surely."

"No." Michael shook his head. "Maybe she was trying to bring more value to her life, by making sure she was remembered for longer than fifteen minutes, not disappearing into small town obscurity. They're all going to be remembered because of this..."

Abby isn't...wasn't that stupid. I placed my head in my hands as fresh tears started to fall; frustrated, angry tears. "I'm fed up trying to understand. I just want to forget."

"Have some more wine. I'll leave you for a bit to get yourself together. Then we can have a chat about my degree show."

I glanced at the mural on the wall, looked back at the glass of wine Michael held up to me. He had a strange smile on his face again. I hesitated, a small voice deep down inside telling me to leave, to get out of this place and never come back. But curiosity and the need for more answers pulled at me.

I took the wine from him. "Thank you."

He stood up, gesturing to the shelves around us. "Feel free to have a look around. Everything here contains a part of the puzzle..." he paused. "Of my degree show."

I watched him leave the room, the door clicking shut behind him. I walked back over to the mural, taking sips of wine to try to calm the unease rising inside. To the left of the mural was a shelf of books and underneath a stack of unmarked DVDs. One was propped up, cover facing forward with the words, PLAY ME, scrawled in red. I glanced back at the closed door, wondering if this was some kind of joke. Had I become part of Michael's show?

I took the DVD off the shelf and walked over to the player.

CHAPTER 24

My heart pounded as I stood waiting for the screen to come alive. Just as the DVD connected, a buzzing started from my bag. I placed my empty wine glass down on the table and fumbled for my phone, one eye still on the screen.

"Hello?" I answered.

"Kat?"

I barely registered the unfamiliar female voice on the other end as a shaky image of Eddison Woods appeared on the monitor; torchlight illuminating a girl walking carefully in the dark, the camera following close behind.

"Kat, is that you?" The female voice at the other end of the phone prompted.

"Yes...who is this?" A strong wave of dizziness washed over me, and I moved to sit on the edge of the table.

"It's Jess. Rob's friend..."

Jess. My heart lurched. Why would she be phoning me? "Is Rob okay?"

"He's fine, he asked me to call you. He's on his way home..."

My attention was drawn to the screen again as the girl turned around and glanced nervously at the camera, her face pale in the half light. *Sophie.* She was wearing a long white dress and a blue velvet jacket. A description from the papers flashed into my head... *Found hanging from a tree, in a beautiful white dress, like an image of an angel already in flight...*

"Kat, did you hear me? Are you okay?"

"Sorry? What?" My head started to spin, a heavy sensation creeping up my legs, like they were turning to jelly. Jess's voice sounded echoey, distant...

"It's important that you stay away from Michael. Wherever you are, go home and stay there. Rob should be back soon and he'll explain everything then."

"Wha...why? I'm...in the Barn..." My tongue felt rubbery, my words rolling together. I glanced at the half-empty wine bottle. I'd only had one glass...why did I feel so woozy?

"Is Michael there?" Jess's voice sounded strained.

"Away...somewhere..." My mind was fogging and I gripped the phone in alarm as faces from the montage appeared to protrude from the wall, features twisting into Picasso-style portraits. What was happening to me?

"Go home now, Kat. Just leave. We think Michael might have had something to do with the suicides...I used to be his girlfriend during high school and he has the ability to get inside your head. He can be unpredictable..."

"Hold on...can't hear..." The phone slid from my hand as I tried to turn the volume up, my head spinning violently. I gripped the edges of the table as Sophie turned to look at the camera full on, the torchlight casting shadows across her face.

Tears glistened in her eyes as she held up a cardboard plaque with the words *Truth is Beauty* written clearly in black. She flipped it over to reveal *Beauty is Truth*.

"I want to be remembered." I could barely make out her muffled voice, the camera microphone not powerful enough to capture crisp sounds. Her eyes looked determined, but hauntingly empty, like Sophie no longer existed. *"Forever."*

"Forever," the voice behind the camera promised. Michael's voice.

I watched in horror as the camera followed her further into the woods, the torch picking out sections of the woodland floor, shining on Sophie's boots, before illuminating a profile shot of her, the lens zooming in closer.

My phone lay at my feet. I tried to reach down but a heavy

sensation gripped at my arms, like I was trapped in a nightmare in which every inch of my body was screaming for me to run, but I couldn't… My muscles felt rubbery and my brain wasn't connecting with my body. The wine. My empty glass lay beside me. My heart skipped a beat as I realised Michael must have drugged me.

The screen blurred in front of me as Sophie turned to the camera again.

"I want to be remembered as someone beautiful and important. What but death gives life meaning? This will mean something."

"That's right, Sophie. I'll make sure this means everything. Your images will be captured for the world to see," Michael promised.

My phone was so close – if only I could dial Sarah… I glared at my foot, willing it to move, but my legs had turned to lead. Panic shot through me as the room started to spin and it felt like my head was disconnecting from my body. Waves of nausea crashed over me. *Rob, please help me. Please come and find me…* I screamed the words over and over in my head, willing him to somehow sense me, know where I was.

The screen buzzed then clicked to black. Silence. I strained to hear voices outside the door. Where was Michael? Why was he doing this? A shrill ring of the telephone started; the pay-phone on the wall. One ring, two rings, three. Why didn't the bug-eyed boy answer? The rings sounded distorted and exaggerated, like a siren screeching through the walls.

An image flashed up on the screen again; Sophie straddling a branch of a tall tree, securing a rope around it.

No. I willed my eyes to close. I didn't want to see this. Images of Abby that night flashed into my mind. I couldn't watch this again.

The door swung open and my stomach lurched. Michael stood in the doorway, a twisted smile on his face, which seemed to extend manically wide, reminding me of the Cheshire cat in *Alice in Wonderland*. He slowly crouched down in front of me, his face in mine, eyes brimming with madness and excitement.

"I'm glad you found the real part of my show." He hit pause on the player, just as Sophie started to secure the noose around her neck.

"It was so easy with most of them," he whispered. "They were so lost by then, so damaged..." His eyes searched mine, then slowly he ran a hand down my cheek. Like a snake slithering down my temple, down to my neck. A surge of terror shot through me as I realised I couldn't move; that I was powerless to resist this maniac.

"How are you feeling, Kat? You look a bit limp." As he picked up my arm, and let it drop like a rag doll, I caught a whiff of his aftershave...*Rob*...a blanket of comfort, like he had arrived to embrace me. For a moment his face began to morph into Rob's, his smile, his eyes...then a glimmer of reality kicked in. He smelled like Rob, like the phonebox. The calls had been from him... *Why?* I wanted to scream, scratch his eyes out. Had he been trying to break me down, so that I would become another one of his 'victims'?

"What...wasintha..." I tried to gesture to the wine glass, to form a coherent sentence, but my words were slurring into nonsense. The room started to tilt dangerously.

"Shhh." He pressed his finger against my lips. "Just a little Ketamine to relax you. You're smarter than your sister so I knew you wouldn't take part in the documentary willingly."

Ketamine? My mind raced, trying to figure out what kind of drug that was, if it could kill me. But I had a feeling there was going to be more to this plan than a simple death.

Michael's face darkened. "And your stupid, naïve sister didn't understand in the end. Thought it was all a game. As if she was part of a film." He stood up, pacing the floor. "I didn't want to have to do it that way, but I knew she wouldn't play along... It took me long enough to persuade her to climb the tree, to say it was an important part of the 'documentary'. Oh, her face, Kat. Such beautiful innocence, like a lamb to the slaughter. When I took away the ladder, the safety net...and ran away into the night..." He laughed, a manic, hollow laugh. "And if you'd been a few minutes earlier, Kat, you would have found me. That was a close one."

As his words sunk in, a screaming rage started inside of me, firing through my veins. A sensation like my heart breaking into a million pieces, as the truth was finally given to me. Abby had wanted to live. A part of me sighed with relief, the truth releasing me from the burden of guilt. But then a wall of grief crashed down around me. She had wanted to live and Michael had taken her from me.

"I'm sorry, Kat." He crouched down again, his face an inch from mine.

"Get…away." The words wouldn't come out strong enough. *I will kill you…*I wanted to scream at him but the words were trapped inside my head, circling around and around so fast I couldn't be sure that my head wasn't spinning in time with them.

"But I want you to be with her. I know you really want that too." His lips curled into a smile. "And having twins – identical twins – as part of my show. Double whammy. Everyone else will pale in comparison. The two beautiful twins, Abby and Kat; you will forever be on the lips of the world…" He reached towards me, his finger running gently along my lips. The panic rose up inside again as an overwhelming tiredness washed over me, like I was being pulled into a deep, deep sleep.

"Come, follow me."

His words echoed, like I was falling into a dark hole, and then everything turned to black.

CHAPTER 25

Ice surged through my body, shocking me into consciousness. I gasped for air and felt the ground slide away under me. Arms were clamped around my waist, dragging me into deeper water. Movement had returned to my arm and I tried to thrust my elbow into Michael's stomach. Confusion fogged my brain as I struggled to piece together where I was.

"Easy, Kitty Kat. Don't make this harder."

I smacked my lips together, trying to loosen up the muscles in my face. "They'll be coming to find me…Jess phoned…she'll have contacted the Police…"

"I saw the last number on your calls. Why do you think I brought you to the loch, the other side of the woods? They'll be running around, looking for a tree. But seeing as I left the *Lady of Shalott* poem lying open in your sister's bedroom this afternoon, I thought this a fitting way for you to go. Did you enjoy reading her journal entries, by the way?"

I ignored his question, not wanting to think about the fact he had been sneaking into my house all of this time. "Don't be an idiot, Michael, they'll know this isn't suicide!" I tried not to dwell on the words of the poem: *A pale, pale, corpse she floated by, deadcold…* Tried to keep the fear from taking hold. It was important I stayed calm. "Rob and Jess will know this was you." At least I had regained control of my words again.

"Rob, Rob, Rob," Michael whined in a childish voice. "Mr Perfect. The fool had no idea that he was a puppet in this game too, just like the rest of them. I knew he would draw them in, make them feel special, then drop them and move on to the next. He broke their hearts, Kitty Kat. Just like he broke my Mum's heart."

"What?" I struggled against his grip, the icy water cutting into my ribs.

"I saw her looks of longing, her drunken slurs towards him. It was disgusting," Michael spat. "Rob used to ignore her, bring girls back and parade them around the house, thinking it would make her leave him alone. Drove her to drink, made my Dad resent her. Tainted her beauty. That's what he does, Kat. He ruins everyone's beauty…I'm just trying to save your beauty."

"Let me go," I screamed in his ear, taking satisfaction at his flinch.

He hesitated, then kissed me on the forehead. "With pleasure. Sleep well, Kitty Kat." As he released his grip I realised too late he was my only chance of survival. Weights in my coat were pulling me down and the effects of the drug hadn't worn off enough to give me proper movement back in my legs. I had no way of staying afloat. I frantically tried to grab at Michael.

"Wait, Michael, no! Please." My calls were pointless; he had already started to swim away, the dim moonlight above illuminating his strokes as he pounded through the water. I should have tried to talk more to him, get him to understand that his Mum couldn't possibly have been interested in Rob, that was just…*wrong*. She probably just adored him as a son and Michael became jealous. Whatever the dynamics of the family, it had clearly affected Michael's mental state. And Rob, what about Rob?

"Where are you, Rob?" I whispered to the night, tears stinging my eyes.

Tipping my head back I held my breath as the loch started to pull me under, blackness and piercing coldness enveloping me. I frantically pulled at the coat, but Michael had zipped it shut and pinned it at the top. The pockets were also tightly pinned, trapping the weights inside. Exhaustion washed over me, the muscles in my arms wasted. Images of the people I loved flashed through my head; my parents, Rob, Sarah…Abby…My lungs felt like they were exploding as I gasped for air. In desperation I waved my arm around, touching the surface, grabbing at nothing.

Hold on sis, he's coming for you. Hold on, a voice whispered in my ear as I floated down, down... A light shone behind my eyes, through the empty void of nothing, a hand reaching out for mine, squeezing. *Hold on...* An image of my sister, circling me in the water, like a mermaid rippling through the darkness, suspending me in light. I felt separated from my body, part of that light.

Pain stung my throat and lungs. My body was on fire, struggling for one last breath. It would be so much easier, just letting go...

Don't give up...then he'll have won. Don't you dare let him win, Kat.

I couldn't let Michael win, couldn't let him get away with this. The anger – that he'd taken her, taken her away from me – burned through me. I kicked hard, one leg responding. Kicked harder, power returning to both arms as I tried to pull myself back up out of the water. But I wasn't strong enough, the weights holding me down, defeating me.

Please help me, I cried silently, the words echoing in my head, as if my sister was shouting too.

And then a body swooped down, arms grabbing me around the waist, pulling me towards the light, pulling me up... Up, up, up we blasted through the surface, the cool air a slap across my face. I clung to the body, choking up water.

"It's okay, I've got you. You're okay."

Rob? His face like a mirage, as if I had died and he had followed me to heaven.

He held me tight, his arms holding me afloat, his cheek pressing against mine.

I coughed up more water, trying to speak.

"Shhh," he held me tighter. "I'll get you to safety. Don't try to speak."

He started to pull me alongside him as he swam, but the weights in my coat slowed us. My body started to shake uncontrollably, my lips trembling violently.

"Weights…in my coat…"

Rob pulled at the top of the coat, the pins sticking it fast.

"That asshole. When I find him…" Rob growled, the anger powering his strength as he ripped the top of the coat open. He pulled at the zip and I wriggled free, relief flowing through my body at the release of the heavy weight.

"M…m…my hero," I stammered, attempting to smile through my shakes.

He cupped my face in his hands, kissing me hard on the lips, nearly causing me to slide back under the water. His lips felt warm and delicious, and thawed the coldness in my body. All sense of where I was fell into oblivion as he held me in his arms.

"You found me," I whispered.

He gently brushed a strand of my hair back from my face. "Always."

As soon as we reached shallow water, Rob lifted me into his arms and carried me to the shore. He gently placed me down onto my feet and I stumbled, grabbing at his arms.

"Are you okay, can you stand?"

"Not really." I shivered.

"You need to get out of this dress…" He started to undo the buttons.

"Hey," I protested, slapping his hand away in a reflex reaction.

He shot me a stern look. "As much as I'm dying to see you naked, this isn't exactly the time or place… I just want you to warm up. Sit down, take your dress off and I'll give you my jumper."

I reluctantly obeyed, watching as he ran over to the edge of the loch to pick up his discarded jacket, jumper and boots. I slowly peeled off my dress, shivering uncontrollably.

Rob knelt down in front of me, gently lifting up my arms as he helped me pull his jumper down over my head. He touched my cheek, his eyes bright with fear and emotion.

"Don't ever scare me like that again," he murmured.

I ran a hand slowly up his arm, his eyes drawing me in, taking me far away from the darkness. Then I noticed he was shivering, his soaking wet t-shirt clinging to his skin. "You're cold too."

"I'm okay." He stood up, pulling on his boots. "There should be an ambulance waiting at the other end of the woods. We should get moving."

I struggled to pull myself up, tiredness seeping into every inch of my body.

Rob scooped me up in his arms, and held me close to him.

"How did you know to look in the loch?" I asked.

"I stopped by your house as soon as I got back, saw Abby's window half open so climbed the tree, found a book propped up on her desk, open at a poem about a woman in a loch – so I followed my gut..."

So Michael's twisted plan to make it look like suicide had ended up saving me.

"How did he get you to come out here?" Rob frowned.

"He drugged me." I clung onto him as he hurried into the woods.

"What?" Rob's eyes sparked with rage, and I felt the muscles tense in his arms. "I'll kill him, Kat. If I get my hands on him, I'll..."

"You'll what?" An amused voice drawled from behind.

Rob spun us both round in the direction of the voice, a piercing light momentarily blinding me. I shielded my eyes and felt Rob's grip tighten as Michael stepped forward, lowering his torch and pointing a hand-held camera at us instead.

"That was very heroic of you, Rob, coming to the rescue. There was me thinking you'd abandoned Kitty Kat, just like you did with the rest of them. What's so special about her?"

I grabbed onto the top of Rob's t-shirt, attempting to hold him back, sensing the rage surging through his body.

"Did you kill the rest of them, Michael? Did you drug them too? Why are you doing this?" Rob spat.

Michael chuckled, stepping closer towards us, camera still recording. "Only Abby I suppose, though she still climbed the tree and tied the noose herself; I just forgot to tell her I wouldn't be leaving her the ladder once I'd filmed the scene. The rest of them didn't need my help. They understood – they wanted to be a part of this. They could see the bigger picture."

Rob edged away, pulling me closer. "I had an interesting talk with Jess. She said you were good at making her feel worthless, explained that her time in hospital when you were together was a suicide attempt and that you were there with her that night, handing her the razor. That you had made some kind of pact but you never went through with it."

Michael tilted the camera down, shaking his head at Rob. "It was never a pact. I just wanted to make Jess feel safe, help her find release."

"Is that why Mum and Dad sent you away that summer? They knew, didn't they? They suspected something wasn't right with you..."

Michael lunged towards us and I dug my nails into Rob's neck in fear, causing him to flinch.

"They're not your parents, they never saw you as their son. Dad hated you and my Mum only wanted to get you into bed, the twisted alcoholic slag that she is..."

I glanced at Rob, seeing the pain playing out on his face.

"And you think I enjoyed that? You think I wanted that kind of attention?"

"You love all the attention, you've always had a pathetic need to be adored." Michael's voice was dripping with contempt. "You loved all your little followers in the Barn. Smile for the camera, Rob. You're the star of my show."

As Michael raised the camera to us, Rob suddenly dropped me on my feet and lunged towards Michael, knocking the camera out of his hands. The two of them started to wrestle.

"Rob, no," I stumbled towards them, trying to pull at him to stop.

They crashed to the ground, punching at one another, grabbing at each other clothes.

"It's all in their journals, in their messages, the pain that you caused them, Rob. The worthlessness they felt when you stopped paying them attention. You're just as big a part of this as me," Michael shouted. He pinned Rob on the ground and I grabbed at Michael's jacket, trying to pull him off. A mixture of emotion was playing out on Rob's face: anger, sadness...guilt?

"It's not your fault," I whispered over Michael's shoulder, trying to get Rob to focus on me. He'd stopped struggling under Michael's grasp and Michael took advantage of his hesitation, crushing his forearm down hard against Rob's windpipe.

"Stop it," I screamed. "Stop!"

Rob tried to push him off, but Michael was too strong. Panic lit up Rob's eyes, as he gasped for breath. I frantically punched at Michael, tried to push him over, dug my nails into his neck but it was as if he was in a trance; immune to pain...immune to any emotion, as Rob struggled beneath him.

"Please," I sobbed. "You've hurt us enough, please..."

"Get the hell off of him."

I stumbled backwards in shock as Callum pounded towards us, full body tackling Michael to the ground, rolling him away from Rob.

Rob sat up, gasping for air, and I hurried to him.

"Are you okay?" I touched his face.

Rob rubbed at his throat, nodding. He stared at Callum in surprise. "Where did you come from?"

"The Barn," a familiar voice answered for him.

I jumped up as Sarah hurried towards me out of the trees, followed by a team of police officers and a couple of paramedics. She grabbed me in a hug and I let her squeeze me half to death.

"I'm so glad you're okay. We went to the Barn and it was locked and Callum kicked the door in. Then we found your phone on the ground in that room with the wine, and I was so worried. Then we heard police sirens and followed the sounds to the woods..."

"I'm okay. Cold and tired. But okay," I smiled shakily, glancing at Callum who still held a struggling Michael tightly in his grip. "Callum kicked the door in, eh?" Despite the situation, I couldn't help but smile. Sarah smiled in response, a dreamy look on her face as she gazed over at Callum in admiration.

A paramedic pulled me back from Sarah, wrapping me in silver foil, asking me questions I could barely process as I watched the police officers grab Michael and secure him in cuffs; Rob explaining the parts he understood.

Callum and Sarah started to fire questions at me, ones I wasn't quite ready to answer. My focus was still on Michael, watching him intently as the police officers started to half drag him through the woods. As if he could sense my gaze, he slowed to a complete stop, turning his head towards me.

"Truth is beauty, beauty is truth," he mouthed.

I shook my head firmly. There was nothing beautiful about this truth. I shut my eyes, allowing the paramedics to lower me onto a stretcher. A warm hand found mine and squeezed. Probably Rob, but maybe my sister; reassuring me that everything was going to be okay.

CHAPTER 26

"So, you leave tomorrow?"

"Yup." I taped up the last of the boxes and surveyed my empty room. It didn't look like mine any more and I was relieved to be saying goodbye.

"Can we come and visit?" Callum sat down on the bed next to Sarah, his hand brushing against hers in a way that displayed such a subtle tenderness that it made my heart give a little kick of happiness for her.

"Of course," I said. "I'm only moving to the City, so we'll see each other lots."

"It won't be the same," Sarah sighed.

"You'll be going to uni there in a few months," I reminded her. "I bet you'll both move to the City in no time."

"Maybe."

I caught the blush and the smile they exchanged and I wondered if they had already discussed the future.

"Call me when you get there?" Sarah hugged me and I nodded.

"This is for you." Callum handed me a paper bag and I looked at it curiously.

I peeked inside and pulled out a cream bun.

He winked. "Mrs Hodge's finest."

He hugged me, lingering a bit and it was okay because I knew he was saying goodbye to a possibility he had once thought about.

I patted him on the back. "See you both soon."

I sat on my bed listening to their retreating footsteps, listened to my parents saying their goodbyes and the front door shutting and then silence.

My arm brushed against the painting that sat against the wall beside my bed. I turned it slowly, tracing a finger around my face, then Abby's; me in darkness, her in light, joined together. Rob's finished painting; a gift I would always cherish.

I closed my eyes, falling back against my duvet, grateful that my parents had realised it was time to move on; that we had to start again somewhere else.

He was waiting for me outside the cemetery gates. My heart still flipped every time I saw him but it no longer scared me, just filled me with so much excitement and anticipation that I thought I might explode.

"Hi." Rob took my hand and pulled me in for a kiss.

"Hi." I smiled at the bouquet of flowers he held in his hand. "You remembered."

He nodded. "White and pink roses. Only the best for Abby."

The cemetery main gates were open but we still chose to squeeze through the gap in the fence.

"So remind me again where your new house is?"

I smiled wryly. "You know."

"I like to hear you say it," he said.

"Ten minutes round the corner from your Art School," I said.

"That's right." He nodded. "And twenty minutes walk away from my new flat. Handy, eh?"

"Hmm," I nodded. "My parents still hate you though." This wasn't much of an exaggeration. Once the whole story of the Barn came out and what had really happened to Abby, they had point blank refused to let me see Rob, even although he had saved my life. Eventually I had wangled occasional meet-ups, but still no late-night dates. I knew Mum was slowly warming to him; Dad would take longer.

"Have you heard from Michael's parents at all?" I asked quietly, knowing that they had been staying in the City during Michael's trial.

"No," Rob shook his head. "And I'm glad of it. Now the Barn has shut down and I've moved out of our old place I feel like I can move on."

Rob had gathered everyone together in the Barn to tell them it was all ending. The police had been all over the place, ordering its shutdown, mainly through pressure from the bad press exposure. The victims' belongings had been recovered from a cupboard in the Marilyn Monroe room and returned to the families after careful analysis. Speculation about a cult circulated in the press, but no one would ever fully grasp the toxic spell Michael had cast. The only concrete crime he could be convicted for was Abby's murder as his confession was captured on tape.

Families of the suicide victims and many others across the town expressed their hate for the Barn and all that it stood for. Abby's missing journal entries outlined her heightening self-doubt, the words Michael spoke eating away at her state of mind. But they also shone of strength, of her hopes for the future. I decided to burn her journals...I felt it was what she would have wanted, like I was putting her pain to rest.

Rob sent out a request to all of the kids to return their Relapse EPs. Michael had mixed the recordings and Sarah and Callum's theory about subliminal messages disturbed us enough that we wanted to see the copies destroyed...just in case.

I squeezed Rob's hand. "I know after everything a part of you will still miss him."

He shrugged, his jaw tightening, a tell-tale sign that I knew meant he was struggling to suppress his emotion. Changing the mood, he tugged at my hand, a smile creeping up his face. "Did you know Tom asked if I could be his honorary big brother?"

"Really? So sweet," I grinned. "Just don't tell Callum."

We turned the corner, down past the Oak tree, and stopped at Abby's grave. Rob placed the roses in the silver vase I had brought and we sat down on the path, looking at her headstone, each of us engaging in our own private conversation with her.

I love you and I miss you every single day. I looked at the photograph I'd placed beside the vase. We were fourteen and I was still blonde and still looked like Abby. It was my way of letting her know that I sort of missed that girl too; that me changing wasn't a sign that I was rejecting her, just a need to find out who I might be without her.

Now I really get to find out who I am without you.

I unfastened her charm bracelet and hooked it around the corner of the frame.

I can feel you when I look at the moon and the stars and I know that you are everywhere and still part of me.

A breeze rustled through the trees, blowing through my hair and against my cheek. I closed my eyes. Abby's kiss goodbye.

I was ready to let her go.

ACKNOWLEDGEMENTS

Over the years there have been many people who have encouraged me to keep writing and I'm grateful to you all.

Thank you to:

Erskine Writers for welcoming me into the group at a young age and building my confidence with writing.

Teachers and friends along the way who told me to keep writing.

The Scottish Association of Writers, and their adjudicators, who have given me encouraging feedback over the years – with special thanks to Janis MacKay who selected *Follow Me* for the TC Farries Award.

Lorna McLaren for listening to my excited chatter when *Follow Me* was forming in my head, and for her enthusiasm for my stories over the years.

Leona McPherson for offering feedback at the early stages and for always supplying me with chocolate and Earl Grey tea during many writing meet ups.

Other readers of my book in the early stages, who offered me helpful feedback and encouragement (it meant a lot!): Elaine Gemmell, Nicola Keane, Julie Mulholland, Rosemary Gemmell. And other friends who have always shown an interest in my writing: Rebecca, Lucy, Jane, Morag, Elaine, Gemma, Claire.

My work mates at SDS for their support.

Weegie Wednesday for introducing me to many inspiring people and for making it possible for my path to cross with that of Keith Charters…

My parents, Rosemary and Simon, and my brother, Philip, who have always been supportive and encouraging of my creative endeavours.

Big thanks to Keith and all at Strident for making my dreams come true by publishing *Follow Me*, and for keeping me involved every step of the way.

Finally, particular thanks to my mum, who has always championed my writing, offered me invaluable feedback and most importantly inspired me and made me believe I (too) could be a published author.